THE CASE  N

THE CASE OF
THE
SECRET ASSASSIN

KEL RICHARDS

M
publishing
CARLISLE, UK

© Kel Richards 1992

First published in the U.K. 1995
by arrangement with Hodder Headline (Australia) Pty Limited

01 00 99 98 97 96 95   7 6 5 4 3 2 1

OM Publishing is an imprint of Send the Light Ltd.,
P.O. Box 300, Carlisle, Cumbria CA3 0QS, U.K.

The right of Kel Richards to be identified as
the Author of this Work has been asserted by him in accordance
with the Copyright, Designs and Patents Act 1988.

The biblical quotation in the prologue is taken from
The Living Bible: A Thought-for-Thought Paraphrase
by Kenneth Taylor. Used by permission.

British Library Cataloguing in Publication Data

Richards, Kel
Case of the Secret Assassin
I. Title
823.914 [F]

ISBN 1-85078-175-3

Typeset in New Zealand by Egan-Reid Limited
and Printed in the U.K. by Cox and Wyman Ltd., Reading

Author's Note

Just as Shakespeare performed in modern dress is still Shakespeare, so history in modern dress is still history. *The Case of the Secret Assassin* is history in modern dress. Despite the telephones, guns, cars and pizzas that you will find in this book, the story is inspired by a recorded historical event. The investigation is fiction, but it is based on an actual event in the middle of the first century AD in a province of the Roman Empire. (Some notes on the historical background will be found at the end of the book.)

Prologue: A Murder Plot

Gazing intently at the Council, Paul began:

'Brothers, I have always lived before God in all good conscience!'

Instantly Ananias the High Priest commanded those close to Paul to slap him on the mouth.

Paul said to him, 'God shall slap you, you whitewashed pig-pen. What kind of judge are you to break the law yourself by ordering me struck like that?'

Those standing near Paul said to him, 'Is that the way to talk to God's High Priest?'

'I didn't realize he was the High Priest, brothers,' Paul replied, 'for the Scriptures say, "Never speak evil of any of your rulers".'

Then Paul thought of something! Part of the Council were Sadducees, and part were Pharisees! So he shouted, 'Brothers, I am a Pharisee, as were all my ancestors! And I am being tried here today because I believe in the resurrection of the dead!'

This divided the Council right down the middle—

the Pharisees against the Sadducees—for the Sadducees say there is no resurrection or angels or even eternal spirit within us, but the Pharisees believe in all of these.

So a great clamour arose. Some of the Jewish leaders jumped up to argue that Paul was all right. 'We see nothing wrong with him,' they shouted. 'Perhaps a spirit or angel spoke to him [there on the Damascus road].'

The shouting grew louder and louder, and the men were tugging at Paul from both sides, pulling him this way and that. Finally the Roman commander, fearing they would tear him apart, ordered his soldiers to take him away from them by force and bring him back to the armory.

That night the Lord stood before Paul and said, 'Don't worry, Paul; just as you have told the people about me here in Jerusalem, so you must also in Rome.'

The next morning some forty or more of the Jews got together and bound themselves by a curse neither to eat nor drink until they had killed Paul! Then they went to the chief priests and elders and told them what they had done.

'Ask the commander to bring Paul back to the Council again,' they requested. 'Pretend you want to ask a few more questions. We will kill him on the way.'

But Paul's nephew got wind of their plan and came to the armory and told Paul.

Paul called one of the officers and said, 'Take this boy to the commander. He has something important to tell him.'

So the officer did, explaining, 'Paul, the prisoner, called me over and asked me to bring this young man to you to tell you something.'

The commander took the boy by the hand, and leading him aside asked, 'What is it you want to tell me, lad?'

'Tomorrow,' he told him, 'the Jews are going to ask you to bring Paul before the Council again, pretending they want to get some more information. But don't do it! There are more than forty men hiding along the road ready to jump him and kill him. They are out there now, expecting you to agree to their request.'

'Don't let a soul know you told me this,' the commander warned the boy as he left. Then the commander called two of his officers and ordered, 'Get 200 soldiers ready to leave for Caesarea at nine o'clock tonight! Take 200 spearmen and 70 mounted cavalry. Give Paul a horse to ride and get him safely to Governor Felix.'

Then he wrote this letter to the governor:

From: Claudius Lysias

To: His Excellency, Governor Felix.

'Greetings!

'This man was seized by the Jews and they were killing him when I sent the soldiers to rescue him, for I learned that he was a Roman citizen. Then I took him to their Council to try to find out what he had done. I soon discovered it was something about their Jewish beliefs, certainly nothing worthy of imprisonment or death. But when I was informed of a plot to kill him, I decided to send him on to you and will tell his accusers to bring their charges before you.'

So that night, as ordered, the soldiers took Paul to Antipatris. They returned to the armory the next morning, leaving him with the cavalry to take him on to Caesarea.

When they arrived in Caesarea, they presented

Paul and the letter to the governor. He read it and then asked Paul where he was from.

'Cilicia,' Paul answered.

'I will hear your case fully when your accusers arrive,' the governor told him, and ordered him kept in the prison in King Herod's palace.

Chapter 1

Looking up from my book I found the words *eeffoc pohs* staring me in the face.

I looked back down at my book, but the long dreary sentences of Justinian's *Corpus Juris Civilis* seemed to swim before my eyes. I slammed the law book closed and waved to the waitress.

'Another cappuccino please Rhoda,' I ordered.

I stared at the plate glass window not far from my table. It was on that window that I could read the words *Coffee Shop* backwards, and it seemed to me that my life was going, if not backwards, then at least in a direction I didn't want.

Whose idea was it for me to study law anyway? It certainly wasn't mine! It was my father who insisted I become a lawyer.

The cappuccino arrived and I paid for it.

'Thank you, gorgeous. What are you doing after you finish here today?'

'Keeping well away from lecherous law students like you,' she said as she walked away.

11

A beautiful girl, that Rhoda, but she could curl her lip in a way that would kill a man stone dead at twenty paces.

A private detective, that's what I wanted to be, not a lawyer. My father had been a private eye when he was younger, but now he insisted I study for a 'respectable profession'.

My friend Dash was a private detective, and he was the model I wanted to follow, not my stuffy old father.

A glance at the clock interrupted my train of thought. Good grief! Was that the time?

I grabbed my books and rushed out into the street. I had to beat the mailman to the office.

Once out of the coffee shop I was galloping across the forum. Surrounding the big open square were the markets, the government buildings and the temples.

Caesarea, being a Roman city, had all the usual Roman temples. I passed the temple of Vespa, with the little motor scooters parked out the front. Next door was the temple of Pasta, its porch filled with the statues of the minor deities—Tortellini, Macaroni, Vermicelli, and the rest.

I reached my father's office, with its brass plate beside the front door reading:

Ben Bartholomew
Attorney at Law

and sprinted up the stairs. Then—disaster! The mailman was coming down the stairs towards me.

But perhaps I wasn't too late. If I could get my hands on the mail before my father there was still a chance.

I flung open the door to the office, and my heart sank. My father was standing in the middle of the room, his back towards me, slowly reading a letter on which I could see the university letterhead.

'Come in Sam,' he said without turning around, 'and close the door behind you.'

'Look Pop, I can explain—' I began.

'You've finally managed to pass your exam in *Jus Gentium* I see. After what—three attempts? On the other hand you appear to have failed your *Jus Civile* exam again.'

'I can explain, Pop.'

'And don't call me "Pop"!'

'Sorry, Pop—I mean, sorry. But I studied this time, I really did.'

'When? In between hanging around coffee shops with your friends and trying to date waitresses?'

'I'm not sure I want to be a lawyer.'

'Solomon says: "A wise son makes a father glad, but a foolish son is a grief to his mother". Rachel and I are worried about you, Sam.'

'Then stop worrying about me. I know what I'm doing. I'm old enough to take care of myself.'

'You are supposed to be an articled clerk in this law office, and a part-time law student, but you don't seem to take either task very seriously.'

'I've told you. . . the law's not for me. I'm only doing it—or trying to do it—to please you and Mom. You know that I want to be a private detective.'

'That's a dangerous and uncertain profession.'

'But you were a private eye years ago Pop—'

'Don't call me "Pop"!'

'—so why can't I do the same?'

'I passed all my law exams first. And that meant that when I gave up the PI game and married your mother, I had a profession to fall back on.'

Our argument was travelling in familiar circles when we were interrupted by a brisk knock on the office door.

'Sorry to barge in like this,' said the knocker, bursting through the doorway before we had a chance to respond to his knock, 'I have a problem that's a touch urgent.'

It was Philip, the blunt-speaking, no-nonsense pastor of the local church.

'Afternoon Ben, afternoon Sam,' he said. 'I have a little matter of attempted murder to place before you.'

'Sit down Philip,' said Pop. 'Tell me all about it. Sam, put on the coffee.'

'Sam should hear this too,' said Philip. 'We'll probably need his help.'

So I forgot the percolator and pulled up a chair.

'It's those hotheads in Jerusalem again,' explained Philip. 'Their first assassination plan having failed they now appear to have cooked up another.'

Philip was referring to the plot to murder Paul of Tarsus, a hero to local Christians, and indeed to Christians throughout the Roman Empire. Forty young men, all students at the Jewish temple of Jerusalem, had sworn to kill him: as a once devout Jew and a former persecutor of Christians who had changed over to the other side, they had a deep hatred of Paul.

The local Roman commander had whisked Paul away to safety at Caesarea, where we had acted as Paul's legal advisers for his appearances at the court of Governor Felix. Now, it appeared, there was a new threat.

'But Paul is locked up in Herod's palace,' protested my father. 'How can they get at him?'

'They couldn't. But someone who specialised in difficult assassinations could.'

'A gangster? A hired hitman?'

'Someone of that sort.'

'So, what have you heard?' asked Ben.

14

'I've just had a phone call from Jerusalem passing on a message from Paul's nephew, young Nathan.

'Apparently he has a contact in this particular group, who call themselves the Forty. With their original plan to ambush Paul having fallen through, and with Felix refusing to return Paul to Jerusalem so they can try again, they have hired a professional gunman to murder Paul for them.'

'Why would they want to do that?'

'Well, you know what passionate young bigots are like. And they did place themselves under a terrible oath, swearing not to eat or drink until Paul dies. They are serious about this.'

'So they need to solve the problem of murdering a man who is safely locked up inside Herod's palace?'

'Exactly. And they believe a professional killer will be able to get into the palace and do the job for them.'

'So, where do Sam and I come in?' asked Ben.

'I want you to take on the case. Just this one time I want you to go back into the detective business.'

'But I'm not a detective now,' protested Ben. 'I've been a lawyer, and nothing but a lawyer, for twenty-four years.'

'That's why I'm suggesting that Sam could help,' said Philip.

'Say yes, Pop, it's a great idea!' I said. 'I can do the leg work, and you can do the brain work. You've got to agree!'

'This is important Ben,' said Philip. 'It's difficult for me to know who to turn to. Cornelius would help of course, but he has his official duties. And anyway, I suspect that this case may well baffle a military man like Cornelius. It will require considerable ingenuity.'

'What exactly do you want me to do?'

'Identify the hired murderer before he has a chance

15

to strike. There may be clues to be found in Jerusalem by investigating the activities of the Forty—Paul's nephew Nathan may be able to help there. Then there is the business of keeping track of the movement of professional criminals in and out of Caesarea.'

'Well, I have practised enough criminal law over the years to have some underworld informers who could help', said my father.

'There you are!' said Philip. 'Only you can do this for us, Ben.'

'Come on, Pop. You and I can do this together,' I added.

Dad turned and looked at me strangely. I thought he was about to say 'Don't call me Pop', but then I realised he was thinking of something else. He may even have been thinking that it would be good for the two of us to do something together that didn't involve me being reluctant and him nagging.

'Okay,' he said. 'We'll take it on—Sam and I.'

A few minutes later, after Philip had left, I turned to my father and said, ' This is great Pop! Where do we start?'

'You just calm down a bit, Sam. I want you to take a long, sober breath and realise how dangerous this investigation could be. Tracking down a professional killer means tracking down someone who won't hesitate to kill to protect himself. At no stage in this investigation are you to take any risks, do you understand me?'

'Sure, Pop. Where do we start?'

'We start in Jerusalem, since that's where the plot is being hatched. I can't get away from the office on such short notice, so I'm sending you to Jerusalem to talk to Nathan and to find out as much as you can about the activities of the Forty.'

16

'When do I leave?'

'First thing tomorrow morning.'

Terrific! Tomorrow was Sunday, and that meant that instead of sitting in church bored out of my brain, I would be off to Jerusalem to start investigating my very first case.

Chapter 2

When we closed up the office, I left Pop to go home ahead of me, while I headed off to visit my friend Dash.

I hurried across town passing all the rows of small shops, half of them wine shops, and half the customers already drunk. I passed through the archway of an aqueduct, its heavy stones covered by the inevitable graffiti saying 'Romans Go Home', 'Free Gaul', and 'Aqueducts Suck'.

As the Caesarea operative of the Continental Detective Agency Dash had a typical private eye's office—a small, sparse second storey office, above a dark and dingy alleyway in the waterfront district.

As I hurried up the last flight of stairs I could see Dash sitting at his desk through the half-open door.

Dash's jaw was long and bony. His yellow-grey eyes were deep set. His wavy hair was grey, and his upper lip carried a trim, military moustache. Dash was an army veteran, and his face had the wrinkled brow and weather-beaten look of the man who has seen too much active service.

'Dash, I've got a case!' I shouted, bursting into the room and pushing the door wide open.

Then I saw the other man in the room.

'Sorry—I didn't know you had a visitor,' I muttered, feeling embarrassed.

'This, I take it, is a friend of yours?' enquired the visitor.

He was younger than Dash, and darker—black hair and eyes—with the sort of distinguished good looks the romantic novelists call "patrician".

'This is Sam Bartholomew, law student and would-be private detective,' said Dash, making the introductions with an amused tone in his voice, 'and this is Publius Camillus, my boss.'

'I'm sorry to burst in like this, sir, I didn't realise that. . . ' I began.

'Think nothing of it, young Bartholomew,' oozed Camillus, in the kind of polished accent that could come from nowhere but the imperial capital itself.

'Publius has just arrived from Rome to spring one of his "surprise visits" on me,' explained Dash.

'To look at the books, check the efficiency of the local office—that sort of thing,' added Camillus.

'I'll come back later then,' I said.

'Not so fast,' said Dash. 'As you exploded through my doorway did you say something about having a case?'

'Yes, out with it, young Bartholomew,' said Camillus. 'You have us intrigued now.'

'Well,' I hesitated for a moment, but I was too full of my news to hold back, 'Pop has been persuaded to take on an investigation and I'm working with him on it, and I'm off to Jerusalem first thing tomorrow to start digging around.'

'And what's the case about?' asked Dash.

19

I explained about Paul, and the Forty, and the hired assassin.

'Jolly interesting I'm sure,' said Camillus, sounding bored.

'Look, Dash,' I said, 'my real reason for coming was to ask for your help. When I get back from Jerusalem with whatever information or clues I manage to dig up I'd like to drop in and talk the case over with you.'

'Sure thing,' said Dash, in his relaxed and amiable manner. 'But right now, Sam, if you don't mind, Publius and I had better get back to these accounts.'

'Right. See you later. Nice to have met you, Mr Camillus.'

I walked back home through the silver chill of twilight. A fine mist of rain had given the sidewalk a polish that reflected the lights on the buildings. Both over my head, and reflected under my feet, was the flashing neon sign of *Caveat Emptor*, the big department store.

As I walked I was honest enough to admit to myself that my real reason for talking the case over with Dash was that I just didn't trust my father to understand the clues or make sense of the puzzles we were bound to run into.

That night, after dinner, I wanted to raise the question of transport. But of course, I had to wait until the young ones were in bed, and the house was quiet. You will understand how rarely our house is quiet when I tell you I am the eldest of five children: after me comes Naomi, then Daniel, and then the twins— Deborah and Tabitha.

Into the peace and quiet that settled on the house after the washing up was done, I cautiously put my question:

'Mom, can I borrow your car to drive to Jerusalem tomorrow?'

I'm always looking for an excuse to get behind the wheel of my Mom's car. It's a fully imported Roman sports car: a six cylinder, three litre Momentum with fuel injection—in Italian racing red, of course. Absolutely awesome!

'What do you think Ben?' asked Mom, turning to Pop.

'Well, Rachel, it's your car,' said Pop thoughtfully, 'but as long as Sam promises to drive carefully I see no reason why not.'

'Thanks Pop, thanks Mom, I'll be careful, I promise.'

'Now, I've arranged for you to stay with your grandma while you're in Jerusalem,' said my father.

'Aw, come on Pop!' I complained.

'Don't call me Pop, and Momma will take very good care of you.'

'And just where did you imagine that you would stay, Sam?' asked my mother.

'I thought I'd rent a room at one of those inns where the hoods and gangsters hang out. That way I'd be on the spot to pick up gossip.'

'Solomon says: "Gossip is so tasty! How we love to swallow it!" Our investigation will not be based on gossip but on facts: on our own observations and deductions,' said my father firmly. 'Furthermore, staying at an underworld inn comes under the heading of unnecessary risks, and is definitely out!'

'But—'

'But me no "buts"! You stay with Momma and that's it!'

'Your father is right, dear, it would be the sensible thing to do.'

At that point I gave up.

You can only reason with parents so far. Parents just don't understand when they're being unreasonable.

And so it was that at nine o'clock the next morning I was gunning a flashing red sports car out of Caesarea, up the slope of the coastal hills, and south east towards Jerusalem.

The car climbed the hills in blazing sunlight, winding between low borders of cactus.

Below me I could see the city—the dazzling Roman metropolis of Caesarea dominated by its three great public buildings: Herod's palace; the huge temple dedicated to Caesar and Rome; and the enormous amphitheatre on which I could read the brightly coloured sign saying The Palladium.

Beyond the palm-fringed city was the magnificent harbour with its stone piers running out into the rocky bay, protected by the artificial breakwaters of granite to the north and south. And beyond the harbour was the brilliant blue of the Mediterranean Sea.

As the road climbed higher I could see to the north and south of the city the great sand hills—looking like miniature mountains of fine gold in the sunlight.

With the engine purring like the deep throated roar of a lion about to spring I sped across the Plain of Sharon, through Antipatris, and up the rocky hillside to Jerusalem.

Less than an hour after leaving the coast I pulled up in front of my grandmother's house. I leapt out of the car, grabbed my travelling bag from the back seat, and knocked on the front door.

'Ah, it's you, Samuel,' she said, opening the door (Grandma is the only one who calls me Samuel). 'You're earlier than I expected. Come in.'

As she led the way upstairs, Grandma—or Momma, as my father calls her—kept chattering away to me.

'I'll put you in your father's old room. It's a room full of memories for me. It's where my own dear Benjamin lived until he married that Rachel woman. She turned him into a Christian! What sort of thing is that to do to a nice Jewish mother like me, I ask you?'

'It wasn't Mom who did that,' I explained. 'Pop investigated the whole thing and decided for himself.'

'That's very loyal of you to say that, Samuel. I like a boy who's loyal to his mother. It's a pity my Benjamin couldn't learn a few lessons from you about loyalty to mothers. And fathers. It killed his father, you know. When Benjamin became a Christian my dear late husband died of a broken heart.'

'Grandma, he was hit by a semi-trailer.'

'That too, but also he had a broken heart. I'm a mother, I know these things.'

I dropped my travelling bag on the bed in Pop's old room, then followed Grandma down stairs to the kitchen for the morning tea she insisted on serving me.

'When Benjamin rang me this morning to say that you were coming, I cooked a few things for you.'

Spread out on the kitchen table was a feast that would feed about a horde-and-a-half of ravenous barbarian Gauls.

'Tuck into the food, Samuel—enjoy, enjoy,' said Grandma.

For the next half hour or so I diligently tried to eat my way through the mountain of finger food that grandma had prepared. At length my stomach admitted defeat, and I pushed my chair back from the table.

'Have another vol-au-vent, Samuel, and some more garlic bread. You need your sustenance.'

'That's very kind of you, Grandma, but I've been sustenanced to the limit. I don't think I'll need to eat again until the middle of the week after next.'

'Very well, Samuel, if you are quite sure you have eaten a sufficiency, you may leave the table.' Grandma still thought I was seven years old, not twenty-two.

'I have to go now, Grandma. I have an appointment to meet our contact man in Jerusalem. I expect I'll be back tonight for dinner.'

I pulled on a jacket, slipped out of Grandma's house, and walked briskly across town, trying to walk off all the food I had eaten.

Our contact in Jerusalem was a man named Mnason—one of the leaders of the Christian church in this most Jewish of cities.

Chapter 3

It was at Mnason's house that Paul himself had stayed during his recent visit to Jerusalem, and it was Mnason that Paul's nephew Nathan had contacted when he learnt of the new threat.

The door was opened by a little gnome of a man—short, squat, bald, and bearded. Mnason was a cabinetmaker and his house was half dwelling, half workshop.

He ushered me in and offered me coffee, which I politely refused—Grandma's cakes and savouries still occupying every available inch of my innards.

'Ben rang me this morning, Sam,' he said, 'and I've been able to arrange a meeting with Nathan, here, at around lunchtime.'

'That sounds fine,' I responded.

Mnason went back to work on a fireplace surround he was making, and for the next hour or so I watched him work while he talked.

His craftsman's fingers flew over the wood—the finest Lebanese cedar—carving, trimming, sanding, polishing with deft and impressive skill.

I wandered around the workshop looking at some of the beautifully and intricately made pieces that were sitting on the workbench.

'You do very good work,' I said. ' These stair posts, are beautiful.'

'That's very kind of you,' said the little man between grunts, as he pushed a plane along the edge of a piece of timber. 'Wood is a wonderful medium to work in, and I find a lot of satisfaction in being creative. God created this beautiful timber that I work in and I honour him by doing my very best and most creative craftsmanship when I work in it.'

It was clear that Mnason, like my father, was a religious fanatic, so I dropped the subject.

Shortly after noon there was a furtive knock on the front door.

Mnason opened it and a heavily cloaked and hooded figure hurried inside, glancing over his shoulder as he did so. The visitor threw back his hood. He was a youngster—no more than sixteen. Mnason introduced us.

'Nathan, this is Sam Bartholomew. Sam, this is Paul's nephew, Nathan.'

We shook hands.

'Would you guys like anything? Tea, coffee, wine?' asked Mnason.

'I can't stay,' said Nathan shaking his head. 'Every minute I spend here is dangerous. And when I tell you about the Forty you'll understand why.'

'Then tell me. Who are they? And why are they so dangerous?'

'They are all students, like me, at Temple College. Of course, most of them are older than me—they're senior students. Almost all of them come from aristocratic Sadducean families. They are religious and political extremists of the worst sort. They believe they're justified in doing almost anything to defend the present regime ruling at the Temple.'

'Including murder?'

'Up to and including murder. They wouldn't hesitate to kill me if they knew I had been here.'

'You're not part of the group?'

'No. But I have a friend who is. Reuben—like me—comes from a middle class Pharisaical family, but he desperately wants to be part of the power group so he hangs around with the Forty. He told me a month ago when they first planned to ambush Uncle Paul.'

'Why?'

'I don't know. Maybe the idea of murder bothered his conscience, Pharisees are much stricter than Sadducees. Maybe just because Paul is my uncle.'

'And now he's told you about a new plot?'

'This time he came and asked to borrow money from me. Apparently this assassin they've hired is very expensive. He's charging 40,000 denarii for the hit, so the members of the Forty have to come up with a thousand each. For most of them, who come from wealthy noble families, this is easy, but it's a struggle for Reuben and so he came and asked to borrow money from me.'

'He wants you to lend him money to murder your own uncle?'

'I'm not sure that he knew what the money was for the first time he asked.'

'When is this hired murderer supposed to strike? Is there any time-table on this thing?'

'Soon. That's all I know. They've been planning this for a month now, so it will be soon.'

'Okay, tell me more about the Forty. I need to get a

handle on these people.'

Nathan suddenly became very twitchy and nervous. 'I'm frightened. If they ever found out that I told anyone what I know. . . ' he started to wrap his cloak about his shoulders as he spoke.

'They won't find out,' I said firmly. 'But I need a name—a meeting place—anything.'

'I can't. It's too dangerous,' said Nathan, standing up to leave. 'I've told you that a professional killer has been hired to murder Uncle Paul. All you need to do now is to keep him safe. That shouldn't be too hard in Herod's palace down in Caesarea.'

'It will be easier if you tell me more.'

'I've got to go. It's dangerous for me to stay any longer.'

Despite my protests, Nathan pulled up the hood of his cloak to hide his face, slipped furtively out of the front door, and was gone.

'Well, what do you make of that?' I said, turning to Mnason.

'I can understand the fear,' said the cabinetmaker. 'Those young men may be wealthy, and they may be aristocrats, but they are also dangerous young thugs.'

'All right then. I don't seem to have got much further. The hiring of the assassin has been confirmed, and I've learned how much he is being paid, but that's about all. So, where do I go from here?'

'May I make a suggestion?' ventured Mnason.

'Please do.'

'Why not call on Claudius Lysias, the Commander of the Roman troops here in Jerusalem. He has his ear to the ground. He may be able to tell you something more about the Forty. And he certainly won't be influenced by fear.'

'But would he be inclined to help?'

'Well, he did last time—when the mob looked like tearing Paul apart. And he whisked Paul away to safety when he heard of the ambush plot. Mind you, he only did it because he discovered that Paul was a Roman citizen. Still, he has helped in the past, and he might help again.'

'Where will I find him?'

'At the Fortress Antonia.'

'Right, I'm on my way.'

I had left Mom's sports car parked at Grandma's place (mainly because I was afraid of denting or scratching it in the heavy traffic of the old city) so I had to grab a cross-town bus to the Fortress.

Although the Fortress Antonia was a military establishment, its office area was just like any other bureaucracy in the world. There were typists sitting at terminal keyboards, looking pretty terminal themselves. And there were clerks doing what all clerks do—leaning on bundles of files, ignoring ringing telephones, while they talked about what they did last night.

'What can I do for you, sir?' asked a snooty young subaltern, in the kind of voice usually employed to address a leprous member of the lower classes of the swamp people of Crete.

'May I see Commander Lysias please?'

'Do you have an appointment, sir?'

'No, but if you'll send in my card, and tell him it's about Paul of Tarsus, I think he'll see me,' I said, handing over one of Pop's business cards as I spoke.

'If you'd like to take a seat, sir, I'll see what I can do.'

I propped myself in a distinctly uncomfortable vinyl chair, and thumbed through an ancient copy of *Roman's Digest* until I was summoned a few minutes later.

'Good afternoon,' said Commander Lysias, looking

up from his desk as I entered, 'but. . . you're. . . '

'I'm not Ben Bartholomew, no. I'm his son, Sam Bartholomew.'

'Take a seat, Sam,' said Lysias, recovering from his initial surprise. 'I've seen your father in court on a number of occasions. He's a brilliant trial lawyer. Now, what's this about Paul of Tarsus? I thought we had him safely out of the hands of the fanatics.'

I told him about the Forty and about the hired assassin plan.

'Well, what can I do to help?' he asked, at the end of my explanation. 'I can take no formal action unless and until this hired hitman strikes. My resources are stretched to the limit as it is. Your best bet is to alert the troops guarding Paul in Herod's palace.'

'That was the very first thing that was done, Commander, and we realise that your hands are tied until a crime is actually committed. But in the meantime, we are doing our best to identify this secret assassin before he strikes.'

'How can I help?'

'Our contact is too frightened of the thugs in the Forty to tell us any more than that this plan is on. I need some sort of lead. Do you know any of the Forty? Have they had any clashes with the law? Who is their leader? Where do they meet? Anything you can tell me will help.'

'They certainly have clashed with the law. Usually for drunken brawling and damage to property when they go out on one of their sprees. Their leader is a young man named Caleb. He's never been arrested himself, so I don't know his surname.'

'Can you give me a description?'

'I've seen him often enough: average height, or, perhaps slightly taller than average, reddish brown hair, solid build, and he has a distinctive V-shaped scar on his left cheek.'

'I'll be able to spot him in a crowd—if I know where to look. Do you know where this Caleb usually hangs out?'

'There are a number of bars where you might find him, but the most likely is a bar and grill in the Temple area called the *Burnt Offering*.'

Chapter 4

It was late afternoon when I found the *Burnt Offering* in a small courtyard, opening off a narrow laneway.

Inside it was as dim as a dungeon on an overcast day.

I walked up to the bar and ordered a drink. 'A Bacardus please.'

'You mean a Bacardi?' said the barman.

'If I want two, I'll ask for them,' I replied. I paid for my drink, found myself a quiet table in the dimmest corner, and settled down to wait.

Over the next two hours I observed that the customers of this particular gin joint were the sort of people who put the 'dis' into 'disreputable'. There were a few young/old women who earned their living in black fishnet stockings, and some tough-looking men whose scars did not come from army service.

At length three young men of around college age ambled in through the front door and made their way to the bar. One of them was slightly above average height, solid build, with reddish-brown hair. This had to be Caleb, I thought, but I wanted to see that V-shaped scar on his left cheek to be sure.

In the dimly lit bar it was difficult to make out any facial features, on top of which the young man was standing with his face heavily shadowed by a green light shade. To get closer I went to the bar and ordered another drink.

From the posture and body language of the three young drinkers it appeared that the man I had my eye on was the leader and the other two were his lackeys. It had to be Caleb.

Then he turned to make a joke to the barman, and there it was—a clearly visible V-shaped scar.

I took my drink back to a corner and tried to be as inconspicuous as possible. My plan was to follow them when they left the bar. For that I had to nurse my drink for as long as possible and remain stone, cold sober.

The three drank for an hour or so before I saw Caleb glance at his watch, say something to his companions, and head for the door.

I gave them a one minute start, then followed them out.

They had already left the small courtyard by the time I stepped out of the *Burnt Offering*. I hurried down the narrow laneway in time to see Caleb and his two companions leaving the alley and turning left.

Our starting point was near the south western corner of the Temple, and for the next half hour the three men I was shadowing led me on a winding, twisting course through the lanes and alleys of the Lower City.

Although night had fallen while I was in the bar, I was able to keep my three targets well in view in the pools of light that splashed out of the windows they passed. The Lower City, as always, smelled of boiled cabbage, stale chicken soup, and uncollected garbage.

At the wall that divides the Lower City from the Upper City, Caleb and his friends passed through an arched doorway beside a tower.

Hurrying to catch up, I followed them through the arch and saw them in the broad street on the other side pass the Roman Theatre and then turn to their left.

My task was now harder. Following the three through the narrow, zig-zag streets of the Lower City was easy, but here in the broad, quiet, well-lit streets of the Upper City I had to take great care not to be spotted.

I kept the three in sight while remaining well back—at least a block and a half behind them. I moved as quietly as I could, and took advantage of every shadow.

At length I saw them stop and knock at the front door of one of the wealthy homes that occupy the Upper City. Whose? I wondered.

The front door opened and Caleb and his friends were admitted.

I approached the house quietly, and began to circle it, looking for a way I could see or hear what was happening inside.

With great stealth I peered cautiously over one of the front window sills. Nothing—the room was empty.

Lifting my feet silently over the cobblestones I made my way around to the side of the house. The window here was a high one, but there was a tree stump that I could climb on to get my eyes up to sill height.

The room I was looking into was a study of some sort. Seated around a table in deep conversation were

Caleb, his two companions, and an older, distinguished looking, grey-haired man.

The older man's face was familiar. Where had I seen him before?

Of course! It was Tertullus, the lawyer. The last time I had seen him had been four weeks ago in Herod's palace in Caesarea. The Temple authorities had hired him to prosecute Paul. And now, here he was again, talking to the leaders of the Forty.

I had to find a way to hear what they were saying!

Tertullus had pulled a slip of paper out of a desk drawer. It looked like a telegram. This he handed around for the other three to read.

I wanted desperately to get my hands on that telegram, and read its message!

From my side of the window glass it was like watching a pantomime: their lips were moving but I couldn't hear a word. The telegram I wanted to get my hands on was now on the table in front of them.

Then there was a stirring of movement. They all pushed back their chairs and stood up. Were Caleb and his friends about to leave again? No, apparently Tertullus had invited his guests to step out into the cool evening air of the courtyard.

Here was a chance to hear some of their conversation. Growing close to the wall of Tertullus's house was a palm tree that towered well over the height of the roof.

I began to climb it. My hands could get a grip but my feet kept slipping. I stepped back onto the ground, took off both my shoes, and tried again.

In a minute I was level with the roof, and easing my weight off the tree, onto the terracotta tiles.

Then, keeping as flat as I could, I slid myself forward to the courtyard edge. Below me, a butler was serving drinks from a silver tray. The courtyard contained a tinkling fountain, exotic flower bushes, and benches carved out of the finest white marble. Clearly, for Tertullus the law business paid bigger dividends than it did for Pop and me!

When the butler left the conversation resumed.

'Now,' said Tertullus, 'has Seth paid his share?'

'I collected it this morning,' replied Caleb.

'And what about Jotham?'

'He's promised to pay up tomorrow.'

'He'd better,' said Tertullus. 'We need the money now.'

'Reuben's the only one who can't seem to raise the cash,' said Caleb, 'and if I have to, I'll make up his contribution—and then take it out of his hide.'

Caleb's two lackeys laughed drunkenly.

Then, a thought occurred to me. While these four were in the courtyard, perhaps I could slip into the study and steal a look at the telegram?

I silently slid back across the roof, and down the tree trunk until I was level with the study window.

Gripping the trunk tightly with my knees I leaned across to the window. It was not locked, and it slid open noiselessly!

I managed to push my weight from the tree trunk to the window ledge. The study was still empty and, to my great good fortune, they had closed the study door.

I slid to the floor. In two paces I was at the table and had the telegram in my hand. But, before I could even glance at a single word I heard their voices booming just outside the door.

Hastily I stuffed the telegram into my pocket and turned to make my escape through the window. I had grabbed the sill and was starting to pull myself up when the study door opened and a voice behind me bellowed, 'Hey you! Stop! Thief!'

Then two strong hands grabbed my ankles and started pulling me back into the room. At the same time I heard Caleb shout, 'You two—get around the outside and head him off—in case he gets away from me!' Caleb had an iron grip on my ankles, and his arms were strong. But sheer panic can give a man strength.

With a mighty tug I pulled my legs free, and, in a kind of recoil action, tumbled through the window, hit the ground outside with a solid thump, scrambled to my feet, and tried to recover my sense of direction.

Then Caleb's two companions—hulking college football players by the look of them—came thundering towards me down the side of the house!

Chapter 5

I looked over my shoulder. A brick wall blocked my retreat. Attack was my only available defence.

Attempting a running tackle on two front row forwards simultaneously is not a procedure I would recommend—unless, of course, you are cornered, desperate, and in fear of your life.

So I tried it.

I put down my head and charged the two, bellowing like a bull as I did so. That they both ended up on the cobblestones, and I clambered over them to freedom was due mainly, I think, to surprise.

Within seconds I was at the front of the house and running down the wide street like an Olympic sprinter pursued by an ill-tempered gladiator. Behind me I could hear the sounds of Caleb and his friends giving chase. My legs were pumping like pistons, and my feet were stinging as they hit the occasional sharp edge on the paving stones.

Instinctively I headed back the way we had come.

Caleb was a bigger man than me with longer legs, and by the time I reached the wall dividing the Upper City from the Lower City he was close behind me.

I dived through the archway in the wall and threw myself towards the narrowest, darkest looking alley winding amongst the slum tenements.

Here, zig-zagging back and forth around sharp corners, knocking over the occasional garbage bin as I ran, I started to put a little extra distance between myself and my pursuers.

At a particularly dark corner I flung myself into the pool of blackness formed by the awning of a shuttered fruit shop.

There I stood for a minute or two, trying to catch my breath, and trying to find, from somewhere, some extra reserves of energy. After a couple of minutes I heard Caleb and his gang calling out to each other.

'No sign of him here. . . '

'Do you think he's gone to earth?'

'He can't be far away—we'll find him. . . '

'You circle around that way—I think we can cut off his retreat.'

They could too, I realised, so I had to keep moving.

As quickly and quietly as I could I moved out of my hiding place, and across the Lower City in the general direction of the busy heart of Jerusalem, hoping to find safety in the crowds.

But it's possible to move quickly, it's possible to move quietly, and, absolutely impossible to do both at once.

There was a bellow behind me of, 'Over this way!' and the chase was on again.

Despite my aching legs and bleeding feet, I just had to keep going. Taking off my shoes to climb the palm tree had seemed like a good idea at the time, now I was wishing I had some solid leather wrapped around my feet.

The hunt continued, until I emerged from among the dingy tenements, into a broad thoroughfare not far from the Hippodrome. I slowed my run to a walk, and looked for a bolt hole to shoot into.

It came in the form of a bar called the *Thirsty Charioteer*. I ducked thankfully into its dark interior, bought a beer at the bar, and seated myself in the corner farthest from the door. I sat there feeling almost like a normal citizen, watching the racecourse touts, trainers and jockeys exchanging gossip over their plates of spaghetti and goblets of rough red.

The icy cold drink in my hand was exactly what I needed, and I was starting to congratulate myself on my escape when a tall shadow loomed in the doorway. It was Caleb! And behind him were his two lackeys.

Keep still, I said to myself, just keep still and out of the way and they won't spot you.

Caleb patrolled the length of the bar, peering into faces. His lackeys ordered drinks from the barman, then all three propped themselves against the bar, apparently having abandoned the search.

I breathed a deep sigh of relief. They'd finish their drinks, and go, and I would be free from danger.

They did finish up their drinks, very quickly, but then the orders Caleb gave the others made it clear that they were as intent as ever on finding me.

'You take the top end of the street,' he said to one, and turning to the other added, 'You start down the lower end—I'll circle around the lane that runs behind these buildings.'

Perhaps it was nervous tension, perhaps it was because I felt so close to escape, whatever the reason, at that moment my arm bumped my beer glass and sent it crashing to the floor.

The noise froze the quiet rumble of voices that had filled the bar, and everyone in the room—including the Caleb gang—looked at me.

'It's him!' one of them shouted.

I leapt out of my seat, took a giant, and very careful, stride over the broken glass, and ran for the back door. It was a swinging door leading into a kitchen. I shouldered my way past Italian waiters juggling plates of spaghetti, through another door, down a narrow corridor, and out into a garbage-filled back lane.

From the noise behind me I knew that my hunters were in close pursuit, so I set off on my sore and stinging feet, running north again, towards the centre of town.

It was dangerous to venture out onto the broad avenue around the Hippodrome, so I retreated once more into the narrow, twisting, back lanes, where the shadows were deep and the obstacles to pursuers many.

After a time I found myself in a small courtyard facing one of those fashionable wine bars and bistros that spring up from time to time for the wealthy to visit when they want to slum in comfort. This one was called *Naboth's Vineyard* .

Hearing footsteps approaching rapidly from around the corner, I ducked hurriedly inside.

What I found was a dramatic contrast to the *Thirsty Charioteer*. Here the patrons were consuming sizzling steaks, with fresh side salads, washed down with crisp white wines. And the floor was covered with straw, in imitation of the true slum bars; but this was clean, freshly harvested straw—not second hand stable straw with its distinctive smell.

41

Thankfully, the lighting was dim. The only light coming from a yellow glow over the bar, and from the spluttering fat candle on each table.

I bought a drink and took it to a table against the back wall. The previous patron had left a copy of the daily, *Acta Diurna* on the table. I picked this up and held it high in front of my face, pretending to read.

Over the top of the page three Vestal Virgin , I saw Caleb and his allies come in, looking flushed in the face, puffed and angry. Obviously, the long chase had done nothing to cool their tempers.

I had a sinking feeling in my stomach that if they found me, a bistro full of customers would do nothing to mitigate the damage I might suffer.

The three of them spread out, and began prowling around the premises, peering into faces. I kept my newspaper firmly in place, and pretended to be deeply absorbed in the stock market reports. Sheep were down but oxen were up I read, clearly it was a bull market.

But I remained more aware of my danger than of what I read. My breathing was shallow and tense.

It was not Caleb himself, but one of his lackeys who searched the end of the bistro where I was seated, and his search was somewhat desultory. He glanced around the tables on either side of me, his eyes sliding carelessly over me and my newspaper. I've made it, I thought.

But I was wrong. He spotted my bare and bleeding feet under the table, and suddenly grunted.

'Over here!' he called, while the customers around me began to buzz angrily.

In a moment Caleb was towering over me. 'We've got you now, thief!' he snarled. 'Hand over that piece of paper you stole.'

42

I had not yet read the telegram that was still jammed in my pocket, and there was no way I was handing it back until I knew what vital message it carried.

I made as if to reach into my pocket, then suddenly leaned forward, lifting the table with all my strength, and pushing it heavily into Caleb's stomach.

He let out a wounded roar, flung the table to one side and charged me.

I ducked, catching only a glancing blow from his fist on my shoulder, and rolled out of the way. Deciding that the floor was the healthiest place for the time being, I kept on rolling, then picked myself up and crawled on all fours behind another row of tables.

Unfortunately, during my rolling progress several tables got upset, including my own, and shortly I became aware of billowing smoke filling the air. As it turned over, each table had tipped its fat, spluttering candle onto the straw-covered floor, and *Naboth's Vineyard* was in the process of going up in flames.

Within moments patrons were shrieking and running for exits, and the place had descended into Pandemonium.

But Caleb and his crew were not letting a little thing like a fire put them off, and continued wading through the burning wreckage in search of me and their precious piece of paper.

I was keeping low, below the smoke and below, I hoped, the gaze of my pursuers. Half slithering, half crawling I moved as quickly as possible towards the front door.

Then they spotted me. 'Over here!'

A moment later they had dragged me to my feet. Tightly held by Caleb's lackeys on both sides, I was facing Caleb himself.

'This is for all the trouble you've caused us tonight,'

he said as he sank a fist deep into my stomach. I doubled up, then collected another blow on the side of the face.

When I straightened up again Caleb had a knife in his hand: a broad-bladed knife with a wickedly sharp-looking edge.

'I'm not asking you to hand over the paper,' he said, 'I intend taking it from your dead body.'

Chapter 6

The fire intervened. Just as I was trying to work out whether it was better to make my peace with God or try to talk my way out of trouble, a heavy beam crashed down from the ceiling.

All four of us were knocked to the floor, with me underneath, and momentarily stunned. But as my head cleared I realised that the other three were scrambling to their feet and heading for the exit. Saving their own lives had become a higher priority than killing me and recovering the telegram.

When I tried to get to my feet and follow them I discovered that I was pinned to the ground by the beam that had felled the four of us, and it was impossible to get enough purchase to move it.

'Help!' I called out, rather feebly, because my lungs were being crushed. 'Help! I'm trapped!'

About then I must have blacked out, from inhaling smoke I suppose, because the next thing I knew strong arms were underneath my shoulders, and strong hands were lifting away the heavy beam.

My rescuers were Roman soldiers. They helped me outside into the cool, clear night air of the courtyard. There was no sign either of Caleb or of his friends—they must have decided it would be healthier for them elsewhere.

After a quick 'You okay now?' the soldiers left me seated on a bench in the courtyard and went back to their work—which was fighting the fire.

The officer-in-charge was Commander Claudius Lysias himself. And what I saw that night was very impressive. It gave me a whole new respect for the Roman genius for organisation.

Claudius snapped out orders, each one clearly thought out, logical and appropriate. And as each order was spoken it was carried out.

'Wake the householders—collect every bucket in the block.' was the order given to a sergeant and three privates. There was no need for Claudius to add, 'And be quick about it,' because they were, as he undoubtedly knew they would be.

Within moments buckets were beginning to pile up in the courtyard, and with dazzling speed they were distributed to a line of soldiers and a bucket brigade begun.

Claudius told his sergeant to take charge of the bucket line and speed it up. The sergeant began to chant orders in a loud, parade ground voice that would curdle milk at twenty paces. It had the desired effect. The buckets swung back and forth along that line quickly and rythmically.

Soon water was pouring onto the fire at the rate of a bucket a second. In a few minutes the blaze started to dwindle. A few minutes more and it had diminished even further.

Then Claudius ordered several of the largest and

strongest of his men to start pulling out the burning beams that would have kept the fire alive. When this was under way he sent four soldiers with wet rags into the now smouldering bistro to beat out the remaining flickering flames.

The whole operation was carried out with military precision. As Claudius gave his orders each of his men snapped into action with the precision of Swiss clockwork.

'That was very impressive,' I said to Claudius once it was clear that the fire was well under control.

'That's our job,' he said modestly. 'As a commander in the Roman army I know that when I give an order it will be obeyed—instantly.'

'Well... all I can say is thank you. You saved my life.'

'At the time we didn't know whose life we were saving,' said Claudius with a smile.

'How come,' I asked, 'the commander of the city is in charge of a small fire-fighting operation like this?'

'I happened to be on duty, and it does the men good to see their commander in action occasionally. Now, tell me Sam, how are you involved, and what do you know about how the fire started?'

So I told him about following Caleb, about the meeting with Tertullus ('That doesn't surprise me,' commented Claudius. 'Tertullus seems not to mind which side of the law he works on.') about being discovered in the act of spying, and about being pursued and attacked by the Caleb crew.

However, I didn't tell him about the telegram in my pocket. That, I decided, was something to keep up my sleeve for the time being.

At length we said goodnight and went our separate ways, Claudius back to the Fortress Antonia, and me to Mnason's house.

I didn't want to give my grandma a fright by turning up at her house in the early hours of the morning in my present dishevelled and disreputable state, so I thought Mnason's house should be my first port of call—to clean up a little and report on the night's events.

It turned out to be a long, slow, weary and dreary walk. My feet were very sore and painful, the muscles in my legs felt as though they had spent the last month running a message from Marathon, and the rest of my body just wanted to sleep. By the time I arrived it was nearly dawn.

It took some minutes of pounding on his front door to rouse Mnason.

'Good grief! What's happened to you, Sam?' he said, as he swung open the door. 'Come in, come in. We'll get some coffee and brandy inside you, and clean up those wounds.'

A few minutes later I was leaning back in Mnason's most comfortable chair, sipping on a large brandy-laced cup of coffee, while the little cabinetmaker fussed around me with washcloths and antiseptic.

And while he fussed over me like the most diligent of nurses, I told the story of my adventures.

When I got to the part about the telegram I suddenly realised that I had still not read the cursed thing. I dug it quickly out of my pocket and read it out loud.

'"On location. Will wire instructions re payment. (Signed) Blackbird". That's what it says, Mnason. And having read it I am none the wiser. What do you think it means?'

'I haven't a clue. Hold still, this may sting a bit.'

'Ouch! It did. Who is "Blackbird"—do you know? It sounds like a nickname of some sort.'

'I guess so. Don't move while I bandage up this ankle.'

'Perhaps it's a code word, not a name?'

'Could be. Why don't you ask Ben?'

'Yes. Perhaps Pop will know. As soon as you've finished I'll call him.'

'No you won't. Not just yet. Do you realise how early it still is? I suggest that you and I have a leisurely breakfast, and then, at a more reasonable hour, you call Ben.'

'Yes, of course you're right. But in the meantime let's hope we can puzzle out the meaning of this telegram. Who is Blackbird? And what does it mean about being "on location"?'

With my wounds all cleaned and patched Mnason went out to the kitchen to prepare breakfast. The smell of hot toast, eggs and sausages reminded me that I was famished.

The weather being unusually mild, Mnason suggested we eat our breakfast on the flat roof of his small house.

Half an hour later we were laying down our knives and forks with satisfied sighs, as we gazed out at a sunrise that could have come straight out of paradise. The eastern sky was as yellow as molten gold, fading to the north-east and south-east into a rich glow as red as port-wine. Below us the Kidron Valley was still in shadow, but further east the hill tops had been spread with the rich, buttery light of sunrise.

'When I look at a scene like this,' said Mnason, 'Do you know what I always say to myself?'

'No idea. Do tell.' I replied.

'I say "Look at that, Mnason: another Masterpiece by God".'

'Hhmmm.'

'You're unimpressed?'

'It's just that I'm not as religious as you and Pop.'

'So you don't believe in God?'

'I wouldn't go so far as that. So what if God created the world? We just need to get on with the job of living in it.'

'What do you imagine it means to call God "Creator"?'

'You obviously have an answer—so tell me.'

'It means that God is two things: Maker and Ruler. It means he is . . . like . . . me being a wood-worker and, say, Lysias being a commander.'

'Fine. But how does that stop me from doing my own thing?'

'God made the world. He rules it and he made us to be rulers of the world under him. But he wants us to use his rules, not our rules. You just can't get on with your life and ignore God. That's not what life is all about. He is the God Who is There. And we have to treat God like God—not like some second cousin from Cairo!'

Mnason paused to draw breath. 'What do you think about that, Sam?'

'I think it's time I rang Pop—he should be awake by now.'

Chapter 7

The phone seemed to ring for a very long time before a sleepy voice at the other end answered it with a barely coherent, 'Hello?'

'That you, Pop?' I said.

'Sam?'

'It's me, Pop.'

'Where are you?'

'I'm calling from Mnason's house in Jerusalem.'

'Mnason's house? At this time of the morning? Didn't you sleep at Momma's last night?'

'I didn't sleep anywhere last night. In fact, I had a most interesting night, all of it very wide awake.'

'Tell me about it,' said Pop, with a resigned sigh.

I did. Starting with the interview with Nathan I gave him a precise account of my investigations.

'It's now perfectly clear to me,' he said at the end of my story, 'why you had no time to sleep! Now, give me the text of that telegram again.'

'It says, "On location. Will wire instructions re

payment. (Signed) Blackbird." It makes no sense at all, does it?'

'It makes sense to me, Sam.'

'It does? I'm amazed. It's just that I never thought that you would. . . that you could. . . or rather, that you. . .'

'No need to explain. All sons underestimate their fathers. But I might have more knowledge than you give me credit for, my son. As Solomon says: "It is foolish to speak scornfully of others".'

I cleared my throat to cover my embarrassment, and said, 'So what do you want me to do next, Pop?'

'Don't call me, Pop. And come straight home. You have done an excellent job, Sam. You have uncovered exactly what we need to know right now. So thank Mnason for me for taking such good care of you, pick up your things from Momma's, and come straight home.'

'Okay. But first—explain what that telegram means.'

'I'll explain when I see you,' he said firmly, and hung up.

I went back up to the roof and reported the conversation to Mnason.

'Ben Bartholomew is as sharp as a Syrian blade,' said Mnason. 'And if anything is going to keep Paul safe from the assassin's hand it will not be—please don't be offended—your strong young muscles, but Ben's wise old brain.'

There was no response I could make to that kind of stuff, so I just passed on Pop's thanks for taking care of me, and asked for another cup of coffee.

When it was a reasonable hour—reasonable to assume that Grandma would be up and about, that is—I said farewell to Mnason and went to collect my things.

52

Grandma answered my knock on her door with a cry of alarm and outrage. 'Samuel! What has happened to you? Come inside, have some breakfast, you look terrible!'

'I've already eaten breakfast, thanks, Grandma,' I explained as I followed her into the house. I felt an urgent need to make this clear from fear of being put through another of Grandma's over-feeding tortures.

'All those bandages and bruises—my poor grandson, what have they done to you?'

I gave her a shortened—and toned-down—version of the night's events.

'But that is utterly terrible Samuel! Being beaten up like that. Just terrible. Are you in pain? Should I get you an aspirin? Maybe two aspirin?'

'I'm fine now thanks, Grandma.'

'You must take better care of yourself, my boy. Even if you don't care about yourself you should think of your poor old grandmother, and your mother, and your father. We all love you and we want that nothing bad should happen to you.'

'I appreciate that, Grandma.'

'Don't interrupt me when I'm lecturing you. You are as bad as your father. It's this detective business, isn't it? Why you should want to play at this detective business I have no idea. Your father, my dear Benjamin, would come home beaten up—regular as clockwork he would come home beaten up, when he was a detective. For your grandma's sake, stay away from being a detective, Samuel my boy. Stay right away from it.'

I promised her I would. All right, it was a lie—but it made her feel better, so is that so bad?

From Grandma's I collected my travelling bag, threw it in the back of Mom's sports car, kissed

53

Grandma goodbye and gunned the car into life.

Before long I was out of the city, heading north-west down the steep slope towards the coastal plain.

I slowed down to pass through the town of Lydda, then picked up speed again. It was one of those clear, hot, dry mornings that are just perfect for driving.

From a high ridge there was a view of the small port of Joppa away on the left, just before the road passed through Antripatris and began to descend steeply again.

Before long I was down on the flat coastal plain, and shooting past Roman milestones that counted down the distance to Caesarea.

Late in the morning I pulled up in front of our house.

Mom was pleased to see me, upset about my injuries, and pleased the car had returned without a scratch. 'If you could just look after yourself as well as you look after my car I would be a much happier mother.'

'It's nothing. I feel fine. Really I do. Where's Pop?'

Mom's attempt at a reply was interrupted by the twins, Deborah and Tabitha.

'Have you been visiting Grandma, Sammy?'

'Why didn't you take us with you?'

'Did Grandma give you anything for us?'

'Did you bring back presents for us from Jerusalem?'

'Children, Sam had no time to buy anyone any presents. You two run along, I'll be with you in a moment,' said Mom. 'Ben's gone to the office, Sam. He said I was to send you there as soon as you arrived. But would you like coffee first?'

'No thanks, Mom. I need to confer with Pop urgently.'

After hurrying across town on my sore feet, I bounded up the stairs and flung open the office door.

Old Zimri, our law clerk, was sorting files.

'Morning, Zee. Is Pop in?'

'Good morning, Mr Samuel,' he quavered. 'Your father is in his office.'

Once in Pop's office I pulled out of my pocket the telegram I had lifted from Tertullus, and laid it on the desk.

'There it is, Pop. What do you make of it?'

'Welcome back, Sam. How was the drive?' he said, as he picked up the telegram, turned it over in his fingers, and read its message.

'Fine. No problems. Now, tell me what that message means.'

'What is your guess, Sam?'

'Well, "Blackbird" must be either a nickname or a code-word I would guess... but apart from that, it has me bamboozled.'

'Over the years,' explained Pop, 'I have done a wide range of law: some conveyancing, wills, contract law, and so on. There's always a lot of litigation in seaports like Caesarea. And amongst all that has been enough criminal law for me to have an ear to the underworld grapevine.'

Pop pushed his chair back from the desk, and leaned back in the padded leather.

'As a result, I know that there are a number of paid killers on hire to the highest bidder around the Empire. And the most feared, the most mysterious, the most secretive of them all operates under the code-name of "Falcon".

'We know that the Forty have employed a hired killer, and that they are being charged a great deal of money—forty thousand denarii, no less. For that money, I would assume they are getting the best: and the Falcon is the best there is. Further, it seems reasonable that the Falcon—with his passion for secrecy—would sign a telegram "Blackbird".

'But how would the Forty have made contact with this Falcon?'

'I imagine Tertullus would have done that for them. He has often done legal work for some of the head men of organised crime in Jerusalem, so it seems reasonable that he would know—or could find out—how to make contact with the Falcon.'

'And the rest of the message—what does that mean?'

'Well, "On location" must surely mean that the Falcon has arrived in Caesarea.'

'You mean he's not based here?'

'Certainly not. He has been known to strike all over the Roman Empire. With such a wide field of operations I would assume that he is based in Rome itself. But now—if the message is to be believed—he is here in this city.'

'And getting ready to strike at Paul?'

'He must at this minute be laying his plans. If, that is, he has not already done so. As for the remainder of the message, "Will wire instructions re payment", that means exactly what it says. As soon as he has worked out how he wants his payment of forty thousand denarii transmitted to him he will send directions.'

'We are going to have to work fast then.'

'We are indeed. However, the Falcon does not kill for pleasure, only for money. That being the case, he will not strike until he has received his payment. Or, at least, until he is certain it is on its way to him. So that gives us a little time.'

'So, what do we do next, Pop?'

'Firstly, find out as much as we can about this

Falcon. The Roman authorities must have in their criminal files some information about how he operates, even though he has never been caught. We will call upon our friend Cornelius and see what we can learn.'

Chapter 8

Zimri placed a phone call to the office of Cornelius, Commander of the Roman forces in Caesarea. Unusually for a Roman soldier, he was a Christian (and a member of the local church).

'Mr Ben Bartholomew calling for Commander Cornelius,' quavered our old clerk into the hand piece, 'Yes, I will wait on.'

Then there was a delay while someone else came on the other end of the line, and then a good deal of saying 'I see,' by Zimri, followed by, 'Nine o'clock in the morning then.'

He put down the receiver and said, 'The commander is out of town all afternoon, Mr Samuel, inspecting some of the outlying barracks, but he will be available—'

'At nine o'clock tomorrow morning. Yes, I heard. Thanks, Zee. Will you tell Pop? I have to nip out and see someone.'

If the next step in our investigation had to wait until morning, I'd have time to confer with Dash—a real private detective.

On the way across town towards Dash's office in the waterfront district, my head was buzzing. A professional murderer who charged forty thousand denarii a hit would clearly be too much for my father to handle.

In the warm afternoon sunlight I walked along the quayside enjoying the colourful spectacle as ships from around the known world were loaded and unloaded by an international babble of sailors.

There were Egyptians, inventors of pyramids; Romans, inventors of pizzas; Greeks, inventors of philosophy; and Phonoecians, inventors of the phone.

In the alley where the office of the Continental Detective Agency was to be found, the door to Dash's second floor office was closed. A note was hung on the door knob saying "Back in 5 Minutes". I knew what that meant: it was a quiet afternoon, so Dash had adjourned to his favourite bar.

Dash tended to favour the *Ad Nauseam*, so that was where I went. And seated at a table near the door were Dash and his visiting boss, Publius Camillus.

'Pull up a chair,' said the private eye. 'Buy you a drink?'

'Not just at the moment, Dash,' I replied. In the past he had talked me into sampling the *Ad Nauseam's* rum and I had suffered for twenty-four hours afterwards.

'Have either of you two heard of a professional killer who goes under the code-name of "Falcon"?' I asked as I sat down.

'Everyone in our business has heard of the Falcon,' said Dash. 'Why do you ask?'

'Because it looks like it's the Falcon that Pop and I have to hunt down.'

Dash gave a low whistle. 'I'm impressed,' he said, 'There are not many people who would care to take on the Falcon.'

'How do you know the Falcon is your man?' asked Camillus.

Taking that question as my cue, I gave a vivid and detailed account of my adventures thus far.

'So, what do you think, Dash?' I asked at the end of my recital.

'In the first place, congratulations, Sam. You have the makings of an excellent detective,' replied Dash.

'Yes, yes, I endorse that,' added Camillus.

'In the second place—both you and Ben are out of your depth.'

'What do you mean?'

'What I mean is that, if you're tangling with the Falcon, you're playing with the big boys. And, quite frankly, I don't think the game is worth the candle.'

'Is it really that dangerous?' I asked.

'If "life threatening" is dangerous, then it's dangerous,' said Camillus.

'Look, Sam,' said Dash, 'If I had the choice between tackling the Falcon, or fighting a horde of Huns, unarmed and single-handed, I'd choose the Huns every time.'

'So you think Pop has got it right—his interpretation of the telegram, I mean?'

'Oh, Ben's got it all worked out perfectly I'd say. It's just that knowing that the Falcon is involved, now would be a good time to go back to drawing up wills for little old ladies.'

'I don't think we can do that. Paul of Tarsus is an

important man in Christian circles, and Pop has undertaken to protect him. I don't think withdrawing from the case is an option.'

'Really? In that case, both you and Ben should draw up your own wills before you investigate any further.'

'You're making me nervous Dash,' I complained.

'I mean to make you nervous. I like you, Sam, and Ben's not a bad old stick-in-the-mud either, and I wouldn't like to see anything unpleasant happen to either of you.'

'Thanks for the warning, I'll pass it on to Pop. But can you tell me anything else? For instance, what does this Falcon look like?'

'No one knows. No one has ever seen him. At least, no one who has lived to talk about it. He arranges his payments so that his clients never see him, and the authorities have never even caught a glimpse of him.'

'Okay—I get the drift. But look, I want to go back over what little we *have* uncovered, to see what you think of it.'

At the end of our conversation, I was puzzled to discover that Dash could add nothing to Pop's deductions. But that was all right, as long as I could have a professional like Dash check them out—that would keep us on the right track.

A short while later I found myself walking home in the twilight again, wrestling with the puzzles that I knew we would have to solve if we were to stop this Falcon from making Paul of Tarsus become his next victim.

For example: if his appearance was unknown, and if he had never been prosecuted then there would be (obviously) no photograph, and no fingerprints, on record. How could we know who we were looking for?

Or where to look? Any of the strangers passing me in the streets might have been the Falcon, and there was no way for me to know.

Looking for the Falcon was like looking for the invisible man.

The next morning at nine o'clock Pop and I headed off to Herod's palace for our meeting with Cornelius.

I had first met Cornelius many years before, when I was still in short pants and he was merely a centurion. Now he was commander of the whole area, which meant he did less work and had the big office with the nice view.

The palace, now occupied by the Roman Governor Felix, had been built by Herod the Great as a summer palace, cooled by the Mediterranean sea breezes and well away from the sweltering summer heat of the Judaean hills. And it had all the earmarks of a summer palace: no formal throne room, no formal courtroom, and no dungeons, but lots of reception rooms and large areas for entertaining.

As the main public building in Caesarea, parts of the palace had been taken over for purposes of public administration. The local HQ of the Roman Army, for example, was in the northern wing. And there we found Cornelius in his spacious office, with its stunning views of the ocean and of distant Mount Carmel, waiting for us.

'Ben Bartholomew, my dear brother, come in. And Sam, nice to see you again,' was his typical hearty greeting. Although pushing sixty, Cornelius had the slim, wiry body of a man who keeps himself in good shape. (In contrast to Pop, with his pudgy, pen-pusher's body!)

Cornelius had a smile as wide as the Nile in flood,

a handshake like a gladiator, and short, crew-cut, steel-grey hair.

As we responded to his warm greeting, we seated ourselves in the comfortable leather chairs facing his desk.

'Now, can I offer you two some coffee? I guess I'm still a Roman at heart because I have a cappuccino machine next door, and my secretary can whip some up in seconds.'

We both said yes, and Cornelius pressed the intercom on his desk and issued the appropriate order.

'Now look at this,' said the commander, 'I've just designed this thing for the army pay office.'

Pop and I must have looked a little bemused.

'It's an electronic abacus,' he explained, 'for calculating the pay of every officer and every soldier, including penalties, overtime, shift allowance, travelling allowance and danger money—right down to the last sestertius—in just seconds.'

Cornelius was gadget mad, and we spent the next few minutes fascinated by his latest gimmick. Then the coffee arrived and the gadget disappeared back into the desk drawer.

'Now,' said the commander, 'what can I do for you?'

'It's about this new threat to Paul's life,' explained Pop.

'Philip has told me about that,' said Cornelius, 'and I have responded by increasing the guard on Paul.'

'Excellent,' said Pop. 'But we must do more than that. We must identify and head-off the hired assassin before he strikes.'

'Yes, Philip also told me that you two were investigating exactly that matter.'

'We are. And, due entirely to Sam's efforts in Jerusalem, we have made some excellent progress.'

Pop then went on to paint a rather highly coloured picture of my exploits in tracking down the Forty. He concluded by identifying the mysterious "Falcon" as the killer hired to murder Paul.

'I see,' said Cornelius, 'Well, I've certainly heard of this Falcon, but I know very little about him. . . However, I know the man who will know. He is my Collator, Smarticus—the cleverest man under my command. His records are sure to have some useful information. I'll introduce you to him.'

'Before you do that, there is one other way in which you could help.'

'Just tell me, dear brother, and I will be happy to do it.'

'Could you arrange for Sam and me to interview every servant who has been on the palace staff for less than four weeks?'

'Nothing simpler,' said Cornelius making a note on his desk calendar, 'If I lined up these interviews for tomorrow morning, how would that be?'

'That would be excellent.'

'Consider it done. Now, come and meet Smarticus.'

Chapter 9

Smarticus's cross-indexed mountain of information was to be found in a dusty attic of Herod's palace.

After making the introductions, and explaining our requirements, Cornelius left us to get on with our research.

Smarticus had the large nose common to certain Roman families, upon which he balanced a pair of spectacles with lens like the bottoms of soft drink bottles.

'Ben Bartholomew, I am delighted by this meeting.' he said, 'Your reputation precedes you.'

'You are much too kind to a humble lawyer,' replied Pop.

'And, Sam Bartholomew, I am pleased to meet you too,' added the Roman Collator. 'Now, it's the Falcon you want to know about? Well, I certainly have a file on that character, although, I confess, a sadly incomplete one.'

He opened and closed several large, wooden filing cabinets, shuffling through bundles of papers as he did so, in a seemingly absent minded manner.

'"Unsolved"—that's the category we want, isn't it?' he muttered. 'Here we are "Murders: Unsolved"—the Falcon will be here somewhere. Let me see now... D, E, F... ah yes, "Falcon". Here's the file.'

'It's a very thin file, I'm sad to see,' said Pop.

'Too true, too true,' clucked Smarticus. 'We only have entries under one heading: *Modus Operandi*.'

'You have no information on the appearance of this Falcon?' asked Pop.

'Oh, we have descriptions that various witnesses have supplied over the past few years. The problem is that if you put them all together you find that the Falcon is a very tall short man, who is narrow, portly, broad-shouldered and thin, with brown, red, black and blond hair, and piercing eyes that are blue, green, hazel or brown.'

'No two descriptions agree?'

'There is no correlation whatsoever between any of the so-called "eyewitness" descriptions.'

'Is the Falcon a master of disguise then?'

'Possibly. Or it might be the case that he has never even been glimpsed in the vicinity of his murders, and hence each description is of some total stranger who happened to be an innocent bystander when one of the Falcon's victims died.'

'And how do his victims die?'

'Often by poison. But not always. There are some knifings that are attributed to the Falcon. And he is notorious for subtle, complex, and devious plans. For instance, I believe that he sometimes likes to manoeuvre a third party into killing his victim for him.'

'How so?'

'Well, this is only speculation mind, but there have been some deaths that underworld rumour attributed to the Falcon, when the direct perpetrator had been convicted and executed. For example, in one case the Falcon was, according to the criminal grapevine, paid to kill a wealthy merchant. That merchant was executed by the state for the murder of an employee he believed (perhaps wrongly) to be his wife's lover. My interpretation of the Falcon's mentality is that he would have enjoyed achieving his goal—the death of the merchant—by planting in that merchant's mind a belief in his wife's infidelity, and leaving events to work themselves out.'

'A strange and devious mentality indeed, Smarticus. You mentioned the use of poison: does this Falcon seem to favour any particular poison.'

'The symptoms in several of the cases suggested arsenic to me. And, of course, arsenic trioxide— common white arsenic—is easily obtained from any copper or lead mine, where it is a by-product of the smelting process.'

'So, arsenic poisoning is one threat we have to watch out for. Have any physical clues ever been recovered from the scene of any of these crimes?'

'I'm afraid not, Ben—if I may call you Ben. Not a weapon, not a single finger-print, not a scrap of fabric from his clothes, not a hair from his head. No physical clues have ever been recovered.'

'Our opponent is clearly a thorough, as well as a clever, man. We must grant that he has a great, if twisted, mind.'

'That's the very devil of it, Ben. Since he kills for money, he can be linked to none of his victims by personal motive. Since he strikes in subtle and devious ways, he can never be linked to his crimes by evidence of method or a particular weapon. He is the hardest type of criminal to catch.'

'Do you know his nationality? Is he Roman? Greek? Jewish? Egyptian? Or what?'

'Again, we simply do not know. At one time there was a strong rumour in the underworld that he was from Malta.'

'A Maltese Falcon?'

'Personally, I never believed that particular rumour.'

'In summary then, we are to look for an invisible man, possibly a master of disguise, who often—but not always—kills with poison, who sometimes prefers to strike indirectly, and whose appearance, nationality, and background are all unknown.'

Smarticus wrinkled his brow and said, 'It makes it rather a pretty problem, doesn't it?'

'That's not how I would have described it,' I interrupted. ' "Impossible" is more the word that springs to my mind.'

'If I may disagree with you, my son,' said Pop. 'I fear that you are guilty of a rush to judgement. Let us wait until we have a larger crop of information before we abandon the harvest. Solomon says: "A sensible man gathers the crops when they are ready". There are more people to whom we have yet to turn for information. Solomon also says: "Get all the advice you can and you will succeed; without it you will fail".'

'But who can tell us more than Smarticus here?' I protested.

'Your son is right, Ben,' said the Roman. 'No law officer anywhere in the Empire has more complete files than these.'

'With all due respect, honoured Smarticus, here you have collated the data which comes to you from your informers. We, on the other hand, can take a more active role. We can actively seek those people who have the information we need. As Solomon says: "People learn from people, just as iron sharpens iron".'

Doubt clouded Smarticus's face as he said, 'I wish you well in your investigations, Ben Bartholomew. If I can help any further, don't hesitate to call on me.'

With that we took our leave of the Collator and his dusty attic.

In the corridor outside the Collator's office Pop turned to me and said, 'While we're here, Sam, we should pay a visit to our client.'

By "client" he meant Paul of Tarsus, and so we headed off for the lower level where Paul was being held under lock and key.

The fact was that Paul was our client in a legal sense, as well as in our capacity as detectives. When he had been hurriedly brought down from Jerusalem a month before, we had consulted with him and helped to prepare his defence.

Five days after Paul's arrival, Tertullus and his client, Ananias the High Priest, arrived, together with a number of other priests and temple authorities, to press their charges. Governor Felix was on the bench in his capacity as High Court judge.

Tertullus was a clever lawyer, and he presented his case in a fawning but effective speech:

'Your Excellency, you have given quietness and peace to us Jews and have greatly reduced the discrimination against us. And for this we are very, very grateful to you. But lest I bore you, kindly give me your attention for only a moment as I briefly outline our case against this man. For we have found him to be a trouble-maker—a perfect pest—a man who is constantly inciting the Jews throughout the entire world to riots and rebellions against the Roman government.

'He is a ringleader of the sect known as the Nazarenes. Moreover, he was trying to defile the Temple when we arrested him.

'We would have given him what he justly deserves, but Lysias, the commander of the garrison, came and took him violently away from us, demanding that he be tried by Roman law. You can find out the truth of our accusations by examining him yourself.'

Paul presented his own defence, with Pop acting as legal counsel and adviser. And his opening address to Felix wasn't too bad at all:

'I know, sir,' said Paul, 'that you have been a judge of Jewish affairs for many years, and this gives me confidence as I make my defence. You can quickly discover that it was no more than twelve days ago that I arrived in Jerusalem to worship at the Temple, and you will discover that I have never incited a riot in any synagogue or on the streets of any city; and these men certainly cannot prove the things they accuse me of doing.

'But one thing I do confess, that I believe in the Way of Salvation, which they refer to as a sect; I follow that system of serving the God of our ancestors; I firmly believe in the Jewish law and everything written in the books of prophecy; and I believe, just as these men do, that there will be a resurrection of both the righteous and the ungodly. Because of this I try with all my strength to always maintain a clear conscience before God and man.

'After several years away, I returned to Jerusalem with money to aid the Jews, and to offer a sacrifice to God. My accusers saw me in the Temple as I was presenting my thank offering. I had shaved my head as their laws required, and there was no crowd around me, and no rioting! But some Jews from Turkey were there (who ought to be here if they have anything against me)—'

At this point Paul's speech was interrupted by loud jeers and catcalls by the mob that had come down from Jerusalem, and Felix had to thump his staff on the floor several times and call the courts to silence.

'But look!' Paul continued. 'Ask these men right here whether their Council found any wrongdoing in me! When I was there all I said was, "I am here before this Council to defend myself for believing that the dead will rise again!"—which gave offence to no one except the Sadducees.'

At this, a great clamour broke out from the Jerusalem crowd, and Felix had to give orders for the public gallery to be cleared.

It was, as I say, quite a good speech. And anyway, Felix knew perfectly well that Christians don't go around starting riots. So he remanded Paul in custody for the case to be heard another day, when Commander Lysias was available to give evidence.

The four weeks since had seen remand after remand. The ruling was always: "Remanded in custody".

Pop's theory was that Felix knew the evidence would not support a "guilty" verdict, but he kept delaying a declaration of "not guilty" in the hope that Paul would offer him a bribe.

In the meantime, Felix ordered Paul to be kept under lock and key, but he instructed the guards to treat him well and not to prevent any of his friends from visiting him or bringing him gifts to make his stay more comfortable.

Chapter 10

Paul's 'prison' was, in fact, a suite of rooms in the northern, or army, wing of the palace. At night Paul slept in this makeshift prison alone, in chains. But during the day the chains were taken off and there was a constant stream of visitors.

Most of these were members of Paul's entourage, who were billeted by church members in town each night, and worked with Paul each day (As well as working on his defence Paul kept up a correspondence with churches he had founded around the rim of the Mediterranean).

The key members of Paul's group at the time were a Greek doctor named Lucas, Paul's two chief assistants Titus and Silas, and another young Greek named Timothy.

As we approached the door that led to Paul's rooms the four guards on duty (until the renewed threat against Paul's life there had been only two) nodded in recognition—Pop and I had been there often.

Beyond the doorway, in a sort of large reception

room, we found, as always, Paul's small group busily at work. In the centre of them was the man whose life we were committed to protect against an ingenious and deadly assassin.

Paul was not a big man, a little below average height in fact. His appearance was even less impressive than usual because of the fringe of grey stubble around the sides and back of his head and covering his cheeks and chin—where he was growing back the beard and hair he had shaved off as part of his devotions in the Temple.

Despite the fact that Paul was physically so plain, he was still—in some inexplicable way—the one person in the room to which my eyes were drawn. Although his eyebrows joined in the middle, and his nose was somewhat hooked, he had a power, a magnetism, and an intensity about him that flashed an unmistakable signal: 'This is someone special'.

When Paul saw us enter he greeted us warmly.

Looking back now, I have to say it was when Paul spoke that he became a commanding presence. As he spoke, his face lit-up (energised by his subject-matter), he sometimes looked like a man, and sometimes he had the face of an angel.

I drifted away as Paul and my father began talking. Generally on these visits to our client I fell into conversation with Timothy, one of Paul's companions, and a young man of about my own age.

I found Tim seated near a window, copying some of Paul's correspondence for wider distribution.

'Hi!,' I said.

'Oh, hi there, Sam', said Tim. 'How goes the investigation?'

'You've heard about it then?'

'Yes, Philip called in here after he had seen you and

Ben, and told us that you two had agreed to do the detective work necessary to protect Paul.'

'Is Paul worried about this latest threat?' I asked.

'Not him,' said Tim with a laugh. 'He says he is immortal until he has completed the work God has given him to do.'

Tim was a very quietly spoken guy, shy almost, you might say, but very likeable with it. We chatted for the best part of an hour while Pop conferred with Paul. Tim was interested in everything I had been doing to track down Paul's would-be killer, so I gave him a detailed account of my exploits.

Soon the conference was over, Pop gave me the nod, and we made our farewells and left.

From Paul's room we made our way down the main sweeping marble staircase to the ground floor. And there, in the vast pillared entrance hall I spotted a familiar face—Dash's boss, Publius Camillus.

At that moment Camillus caught sight of me, and much to my surprise, beckoned me to join him.

'I'll catch you later, Pop', I said. 'There's a guy I want to see.'

'Don't call me Pop! And I'll see you at home for lunch—after which we have another important visit to make.'

'Yeah, sure,' I said, hardly hearing his words, as I hurried away to where Camillus stood amongst a group of officials.

As I approached, Camillus left the group, took me by an elbow, and led me to one side.

'I didn't expect to see you here,' I said.

'Courtesy call,' the Roman explained. 'As a member of one of the noble families it is expected that when I visit the provinces I will call on the local Governor.

And it's good for business to keep up these official contacts. At any rate, Sam, I'm glad I've run into you. There's something I'd like to discuss with you.'

'I'm all ears. What is it?'

'Not here. We need an opportunity to talk at leisure—and in private. I have a busy schedule, so I suggest later this afternoon in the agency office. Let's say between five and five-thirty. Can you make it?'

'Sure. I'll be there.'

'Fine. We'll talk then,' said Camillus, and he started to move away.

'But...,' I said, 'can't you give me some hint of what it's about?'

'I suppose you're entitled to that,' said the Roman turning back with a smile on his face. 'The simple fact is, Sam, that I was very impressed by the work you did in Jerusalem, and I think you have the makings of a fine detective. Now, as it so happens, I have been considering expanding our Caesarean office for some time—and if we can come to a mutually satisfactory agreement, I think I'll be able to see my way clear to making you a firm job offer.'

I was too stunned to make an immediate reply.

'Now I must be off, there are people waiting for me,' said Camillus, as he moved away.

I stood there for a moment, rooted to the spot, completely oblivious of the splendour of my surroundings—the soaring columns, the marble paving, the golden bands of sunlight spilling through the archways.

The Continental Detective Agency was one of the biggest in the Empire. This Publius Camillus could be no fool if he was its head. And this man had spotted some real detective talent in *me*!

I felt a surge of hope in my heart. No more study! No more law books! And I hurried home feeling lighter, and happier than I had for months.

At home I found chicken soup and bagels waiting for me.

'So, what are you two planning to do this afternoon?' asked Mom as we ate.

'Now you mustn't worry about this, Rachel,' said Pop, swallowing a mouthful of bagel, 'but this afternoon Sam and I are paying a visit to the Fat Man.'

'Ben, are you sure that's wise? Are you sure it's safe?'

Even I had heard of the Fat Man—everyone had heard of the Fat Man. According to the rumour mills of Caesarea the Fat Man was the Mr Big of organised crime. He either financed, organised, permitted, or knew about every illegal activity in the city.

The waterfront was the hub of crime in Caesarea, and, as a port city, smuggling contraband was the main illegal profit generator. For this to happen there were sailors, captains, cargo handlers and harbour masters to be bribed or suborned by the paymasters and standover men employed by the Fat Man.

Any petty crook who went into business on a freelance basis would find himself with all his fingers broken unless he agreed to pay the Fat Man a rake-off.

All of which meant there were good reasons for Mom's question.

'It'll be safe enough, Rachel my dear. The Fat Man holds no particular grudge against me. And I think he will be interested in the news I have for him.'

'What news is that?'

'That the Falcon is now operating on his territory.'

'Surely the Fat Man would already know that?' I said. 'He sits like a spider at the centre of a web of underworld information: how could he not know that the Falcon is in Caesarea?'

'I suggest Sam,' said Pop, 'that the Falcon must operate quite separately from the usual criminal world. He must move into a city, make his kill, and move out again with the minimum of contact with the professional criminals of that city. If it were not so there would have been much more information in Smarticus's files. Such secrecy is possible only for someone who is not part of the underworld mainstream.'

'Ah, yes—that makes sense. So the Falcon must avoid all contact with ordinary crims?'

'As much as possible he would. Some contact may be essential—in order to expedite his operation in a city with which he is unfamiliar. That is what I am counting on in my approach to the Fat Man.'

Chapter 11

After lunch Pop and I caught a cab to the hills on the eastern escarpment above the city. It was here, facing the cool sea breezes, that the wealthiest merchants and Roman officials built their splendid villas. And it was here that the Fat Man lived in high-security luxury.

The great, fat spider at the centre of Caesarea's underworld web had become a complete recluse in his hilltop mansion. His henchmen bustled in and out all day, reporting the latest information or gossip, getting their orders, carrying out his instructions, and carrying back the profits of many criminal enterprises; while the man himself lived a secure, and sybaritic, lifestyle behind high walls.

Beside the iron gates at the front of the villa was an intercom. Pop pressed the button.

'Yeah? Who's that?' came the snarled reply, compressed by the intercom into the squeak of a dyspeptic mouse.

'Ben Bartholomew here. I am requesting permission to speak to your boss.'

'Hang on,' squeaked the ill-tempered rodent in reply.

As we stood there on the road, waiting for the Fat Man's lackey to buzz back with a reply to Pop's message, I passed on the warning Dash and Camillus had given me about tangling with the Falcon.

'So—they believe that what we are doing is dangerous, do they?' said Pop.

'They sure do,' I explained. 'Dash said that he just wouldn't take on any case involving the Falcon. And Camillus seemed to think that investigating the Falcon was likely to be fatal.'

'They are, of course, not wrong,' said Pop, 'I absolutely endorse their dire warnings.'

'Then why are we doing it Pop?'

'Just because something is dangerous is no reason not to do it—it is a reason to do it veeeery carefully.'

'But what chance do we two have against an operator like the Falcon?'

'It is true that we are not the biggest risk the Falcon has ever faced. That, however, does not suggest that we shall not succeed. The Falcon's biggest enemy is not us, it is. . . himself. Solomon says: "A man guilty of murder is digging his own grave as fast as he can". If we can match the Falcon's low cunning with high intelligence, if we can match his evil intentions with our good purpose, then we shall be able to bury his current murder plot.'

A series of loud clanking noises signalled the opening of the iron gate that stood before us. It swung back just far enough to let one person pass through. One of the Fat Man's hoodlums stepped out, carrying a gun in his hand, and looked up and down the road.

When he was satisfied there was no one else about, he glared suspiciously at Pop and me.

'Who's this?' he growled, waving his gun in my direction.

'This is my law clerk,—my son Sam.'

'I guess it's all right,' he grumbled, and stood back to wave us in through the gate with his gun.

Once we were inside, the gate was closed and locked behind us, and a second hoodlum searched us both for weapons. When they were satisfied that we were clean, they led us through a splendid ornamental garden and up the wide front steps of a villa built of gleaming white Carrara marble.

The house was like a labyrinth, with carpeted corridors leading off to various wings.

After passing through several locked doors, we were admitted to a palatial office, large enough for a high-ranking Roman proconsul.

In the middle of this football-field of a room was a massive desk made from highly polished Lebanese cedar. And seated behind the desk was a massive man.

The Fat Man was flabbily fat, with bulbous cheeks and lips and chins and neck. When he moved, all his bulbs moved separately, quivering with each gesture.

'Ben Bartholomew, it is a delight to see you again, sir,' he rumbled, in a voice like a tip-truck unloading gravel. 'It is some time since you have been employed to prosecute any of my... ah, shall we say, staff? Some time indeed. But you have always been an honest and forthright opponent sir, and that is why I like you. Please be seated, and make yourselves comfortable.'

We seated ourselves in the plush, velvet-covered

chairs that two of the attendant hoodlums pushed into place for us.

'And this, I take it, is your son?' asked the expensively dressed, quivering mass behind the desk.

'Yes, indeed,' replied, 'I have the honour to introduce my son Sam.'

'I am delighted to meet you, young sir,' rumbled the Fat Man, without, however, offering to shake my hand, 'If you are anything at all like your father then you will be a most intriguing and unusual person to deal with.'

I was surprised to discover that an underworld heavy regarded Pop with this slightly fearful respect.

'And may I introduce you gentlemen to my daughter,' he continued. 'This is Rhea—the delight of my declining years.'

As he spoke he gestured towards a young woman sitting at the side of his desk with a shorthand notebook on her lap. She was dark haired, and brown eyed, and stunningly beautiful! She was even lovelier than Rhoda the waitress.

When the fat man made his introduction she looked up at Pop and me, but she didn't smile—she merely gazed at us coldly.

'Can I offer you some of my hospitality, sirs? A glass of whisky perhaps? A cigar? No? Well, then, down to business. What brings you to my humble abode?'

'The exchange of information,' said Pop. 'I have some information that may be of interest to you. And I am asking for some information in return.'

'Very well, sir,' purred the Fat Man, 'we shall trade. And you shall begin.'

'My information is this: the Falcon is in Caesarea.'

'On a job?'

'As you say—on a job.'

There was a short silence as our host contemplated this information.

Then he began to chuckle, 'You surprise me, sir,' said the Fat Man, all his bulbs bouncing as he laughed. 'That you, an upright and honest citizen, should have this information before me, with my network of spies and informers, surprises me a good deal. Are you certain of your information?'

'Quite certain. Would I be here otherwise?'

'Indeed! A good point, sir, a good point,' and the Fat Man chuckled again, 'Well, there must be more. Who is his target this time?'

'A leader of the Christian community. A man named Paul of Tarsus.'

'And why should this concern me?'

'Are you not concerned with everything that happens in the Caesarean underworld? Can the Empire's most notorious hitman enter your territory and you not be concerned?'

The Fat Man laughed again as he said, 'By Gad, sir, you're a character, that you are! Your ability to understand the way my mind works is quite uncanny!'

'The Falcon's employers are a group of fanatics in Jerusalem who have sworn to see Paul die. They contacted the Falcon some time in the last four weeks, and they have now received a signal from him to the effect that he is "on location".'

'Yes, yes, I know how this Falcon works,' said the Fat Man as he took a white handkerchief from his pocket and wiped his eyes. 'That signal means that he is ready to strike and expects his payment to be delivered.'

'So,' said Pop, 'I am right in thinking that the arrival of the Falcon in this city is news to you?'

'Yes indeed, sir. It is quite new information, and I thank you for it.'

The man's eyes were made small by the puffs of fat that surrounded them, and, as he sat in a heavy, wheezing silence they narrowed to even smaller slits as an expression of intense concentration passed over his face.

'What use I shall make of this information,' he said, 'I do not know. But I intend giving the matter very careful thought.'

At that moment a thin, weasel-faced young man burst into the office through a side door.

'Boss, I got some. . . ' he began in a nasal voice.

'Not now!' snarled the Fat Man gruffly, 'Can't you see I'm engaged? Whatever you have will wait until our visitors have left!'

The young gunsel sat down obediently on a chair against the back wall, his face a silent snarl of disapproval.

'And now, sir. It is, I believe, time that we traded information. You have told me what you know, what is it you want from me?'

'The intended victim is being held prisoner in Herod's Palace.'

'As safe a place as one could want, I imagine.'

'Indeed. Hence, the Falcon's biggest problem in this case is finding the opportunity to kill. To do that, he needs to gain access to the palace. What I suspect you may be able to tell me is how he would go about that. Who, in the underworld in Caesarea, specialises in dealings with palace staff?'

'What sort of dealings?'

'There will undoubtedly be some sort of black market involving the palace. Not all the luxuries the Governor orders from Rome will end up on the

Governor's table. A percentage of them will be side-tracked and turned into cash on the black market. And whoever is running such a scam, will be paying you for the privilege of doing so. Who is it?'

'Why do you ask, sir? I need to understand precisely what you want to know.'

'When the Falcon arrived in Caesarea he will have begun by searching for ways to obtain entrance to the palace—particularly to the palace kitchens, since poison is his preferred mode of operation. He would have enquired in all the underworld bars for a black marketeer who has good "back door" connections at the palace kitchens. He would be looking for someone whose connections are good enough to get him in, perhaps working in the kitchens, so that he can be in a position to strike.'

'I do see your point, sir. I see it entirely.'

'So—who would he have been directed to? That is the information I want in return from you.'

'Not an unreasonable request—not unreasonable at all. Let us say that I suggest you look for an Egyptian. He operates under the name of Mr Cairo—no doubt not his real name, merely a nickname acquired by dint of his origin. Nevertheless, that is the name under which he is known, and under which you will find him.'

The Fat Man scribbled an address on a small piece of paper, using a pen that was dwarfed by his bulbous, pink, flabby hand. This note he handed to his daughter Rhea, who, in turn, passed it over to Pop.

As she walked around the desk to pass on the note she moved with a kind of sensuous shimmer that made it almost impossible for me to concentrate on what was said next.

'Now, in recommending that you speak to Mr

Cairo, you are to understand that I am accusing that Egyptian gentleman of no wrongdoing, and of no criminal activities. It is important that you do not make unfair use of the information I am giving you.'

'You have my word on that.'

'Your word is good enough, Mr Bartholomew, the word of a gentleman and a scholar!'

Chapter 12

Apart from the formalities, that concluded our negotiations and we were shown out of the villa the way we had come.

Standing outside the iron front gate again, by the side of that broad, quiet, wealthy suburban street, I turned to Pop and asked, 'Well, is that what we wanted to learn?'

'That is exactly what we wanted to learn,' he replied. 'And we will follow up the information by making our way almost immediately to the premises of Mr Cairo.'

We had to walk some blocks down the hill before we found a cruising cab. And as we walked, we talked.

'Who was that young tough who burst into the room during our meeting?' I asked.

'He is the Fat Man's chief killer. The Fat Man calls him an "enforcer", although in underworld slang he is called a "gunsel".'

'What's his name?'

"He is yet another whose real name is unknown. As

with all great ports, a deal of flotsam washes up on the shores of Caesarea, people who have pasts they wish to forget. The real names of such persons are rarely known. This particular gunsel is known only by the initials WC. I would add that WC is one of the most feared men in the Caesarean underworld.'

'What does "WC" stand for?'

'It stands for what you would expect—water closet. It is a reference,' explained Pop, 'to his way of disposing of his victims. As you know, underneath this city is a vast network of sewer tunnels, many of them large enough to allow a man to walk erect. They are a typical piece of Roman sanitary engineering gone mad! These tunnels are often used by smugglers unloading contraband, since they all open into the harbour. Well, all of WC's victims are found in those sewers—with their arms, legs and head severed.'

'Ugh!' I grimaced.

'Hence the fear that young man evokes in criminal circles, and hence also his unusual nickname: WC flushes his victims down the sewers.'

At that point a taxi cruised past, we hailed it, hopped in, and Pop gave the address of our office.

'Did I detect a note of stirring in the information you gave the Fat Man?' I enquired, as the taxi carried us towards our destination.

'What can you possible mean, my son?' asked Pop, with a sly smile.

'I mean, by telling the Fat Man that the most notorious hired killer in the Empire is now operating on his turf, were you attempting to stir up some sort of rivalry between them?'

'Solomon says: "Churn milk and you get butter". The more difficult life is for the Falcon, the easier our task will become.'

'I see. And there's one other thing that's been bothering me, Pop.'

'Namely?'

'How are we going to get this Mr Cairo to co-operate with our enquiries? With the Fat Man you could trade information, what can you trade with this blackmarketeer?'

'There is only one language that people like Mr Cairo speak, the language of money. Any information he provides will be paid for in coin of the realm.'

The taxi drew up in front of the office, Pop paid off the driver, and as we walked upstairs I asked: 'Why have we come back here, Pop? I thought we were going straight to see Mr Cairo?'

'Well, Paul is scheduled to make another court appearance tomorrow, and he and I decided today that, in the light of all that is happening, it would be easier all round if that appearance could be delayed. With that in view we have to file an official application for a continuance.'

We walked into our office to find Zimri, as always, diligently at work at his desk.

'Any messages?' asked Pop.

'There are several Mr Benjamin—I have put them on your desk.'

'Thank you, Zimri. And would you bring me a Continuance Application form please?'

'Right away, Mr Benjamin.'

Pop filled in the appropriate details on the form, and then signed and sealed it. Then he read through the messages Zee had left on his desk.

'Sam, I have to meet one of our clients this afternoon—an urgent contract matter. Can I rely on you to lodge this Continuance Application for Paul?'

'Sure thing, Pop—leave it to me.'

'It must be lodged at the court office at the palace before close of business at six this evening. If you miss that deadline, Paul will have to make a court appearance tomorrow for which neither of us is prepared. So you understand the importance of this task?'

'Pop—trust me. Lodging the Continuance Application is simple. I'll do it—okay? But do we visit Mr Cairo first?

'We do indeed. In fact, we do so without delay. Zimri, I'll be back in an hour. And while I'm out, call Hiram Levi and make an appointment for five o'clock.'

To get to Mr Cairo's premises we had to pass through the heart of town to the waterfront, and through those crowded streets walking was as fast as a cab.

We passed the scores of little shops that filled every street, many of them wine bars, and many of those filled with drunken sailors and waterfront workers.

From one wine bar came the awful sound of a sloshed sailor bawling out a sentimental song: 'Wherever I wander, there's no place like Rome!' he bellowed in an off-key, drunken slur.

We passed a large apothecary's shop with its well known advertising slogan flashing outside: 'Lotsa Nostrums!'

When we came to a bank Pop said: 'I had better withdraw some cash so that we have enough in hand to do business with Mr Cairo.'

Inside Pop walked up to the bench against the side wall and began filling out a withdrawal form. He seemed to have difficulty concentrating on what he was doing. He kept looking sideways at what the young man next to him was writing.

As the young man left the bench Pop turned around

suddenly and bumped heavily into him, sending the young man sprawling across the floor.

'So sorry! Most clumsy!' said Pop, and then to me added, 'Grab his weapon, Sam!'

It took me but a second to recover my wits and realise what was happening. I pinned the young man to the floor and then took away the weapon that was bulging under his toga.

As staff and customers realised that a bank robbery was being foiled several screamed, and someone pressed an alarm bell. Within minutes two armed officers of the city watch had arrived and the young would-be thief was under arrest.

As he was being handcuffed, Pop extracted a note from the man's right hand.

'This is the note I saw him writing,' he explained, and then read the message out loud: *Catapultam habeo. Nisi pecuniam omnem mihi dabis, ad caput tuum saxa immane mittam* .

'Translate please, Pop,' I asked.

'It says: "I have a catapult. Give me all the money, or you will have rocks in your head".'

After thanks and congratulations, Pop made his withdrawal of cash, we left the bank, and continued across town.

We crossed the Forum and plunged into the network of narrow streets on the other side. As we neared the waterfront, the pedestrians around us became less pedestrian and more colourful: a collection of barely honest types from around the known world.

On the other side of town the wine bars were called names like the *Amicus*; they sold the sort of drinks that made you feel friendly; on this side of town the bars had names like the *Apocalypsis* , and their drinks made you feel the end of the world had come.

We found Mr Cairo's dingy office upstairs above a bar called the *Rigor Mortis* (which sold really stiff drinks).

'Come in please,' was the response to our knock.

Mr Cairo was a short, small-boned, dark man. His hair was black and smooth and very glossy. There was a cloud of some Gaulish fragrance that floated about his person. His voice was strangely light and sibilant.

'What can I do for you gentlemen?' he asked.

'We have it on good authority,' said Pop, dropping into an uncharacteristically furtive tone of voice, 'that you have excellent "connections". . . if I can use that word. . . at Herod's palace.'

'And what exactly is your authority for assuming that?' asked Cairo suspiciously.

'The Fat Man sent us to you.'

'Ah, well,' said the Egyptian, his face clearing. 'There can be no better authority. In what way may I be of use to you?'

'Suppose,' said Pop, 'suppose that—for reasons I need not go into immediately—I wanted to place an agent inside the palace. Would you, and your "connections", be able to obtain employment for my agent on the palace staff?'

'Nothing could be simpler,' hissed Cairo. 'For a consideration, of course.'

'Of course.'

'And in addition to my fee—an extremely modest fee I promise you—there would have to be certain payments made.'

'And upon making those payments?'

'I could have your agent employed in any department in the palace that you chose.'

'You are—as was promised—a man of considerable influence, Mr Cairo.'

'You flatter me, sir. I am simply a businessman selling my services to anyone who can pay my price.'

'And your price would be. . .?'

'Let us say—one thousand denarii.'

'Not cheap.'

'But an exclusive service,' said Cairo, 'that I alone in Caesarea can offer.'

Pop pulled a money bag out of his belt and spilled a pile of silver denarii across Cairo's desk.

'That is music to my ears,' said the Egyptian. 'I love to hear the tinkle of coins on my desk.'

'But before you pick them up,' said Pop, 'you must earn them. *This* money is on offer in return for information.'

'What information?' asked Cairo, suddenly suspicious again.

'The service I just described—that of obtaining employment in the palace—you have recently performed for another person. Tell me who, and the money is yours.'

'But what you ask is impossible! I must protect the confidentiality of my clients!'

'You are a businessman, Mr Cairo, and I wish to buy your confidentiality. What is the price?'

'Your proposal alarms me, sir. You come to me pretending you want to place someone inside the palace, and when I tell you I can do that, you change your mind and want to know who I have already done it for! How do I know that you are not agents of the city watch?'

'We are not official agents,' said Pop, 'and we really have just come from the Fat Man. If you don't believe us—telephone him and check.'

'That won't be necessary,' said Cairo, sweating profusely at the thought of speaking directly to the Fat

Man, 'I believe you. But you must tell me your reason for wanting this information. Without that I refuse to speak.'

'Very well,' said Pop, and explained about the arrival of the Falcon in Caesarea, and our commission to protect Paul of Tarsus from the Falcon's deadly claws.

'And you believe,' said Cairo, 'that the person for whom I recently gained entry to the palace is this Falcon?'

'So there is such a person!' said Pop. 'We will pay generously for that information.'

'Time,' said the Egyptian. 'I must have time to think. And to make some enquiries of my of my own.'

'Will you help us?'

'Yes—I certainly will!' said Cairo, his face suddenly clearing, as if he had come to some decision. 'I will help you. My price has doubled—two thousand denarii, and furthermore, you must wait twenty-four hours for the information you seek.'

We argued for some time, but that was the best deal we could get, and we had to settle for it.

Chapter 13

Outside Mr Cairo's premises Pop and I parted, he to
return to the office, and I to keep my appointment with
Publius Camillus.

'Don't forget about the Continuance Application,'
said Pop as he hurried away.

'Trust me!' I yelled after him, and then set off for the
Continental Detective Agency, where I found Camillus
in the office alone.

'Dash not here?' I asked.

'I thought it best that we have this conversation in
private,' said Camillus. 'I've asked him to step out for
a little while. Please pull up a chair.'

I sat down in a stiff-backed wooden chair that had
seen better days, while Camillus faced me across
Dash's untidy desk.

'In the first place,' he said, 'I have to pay tribute to
Dash, and the work he has done in building up this
branch.'

Fine, fine, I thought, just get on with it—what about
the job?

'Of course,' Camillus intoned, 'in a port city like Caesarea one would expect a brisk trade in our business. But it has been the flair, and success, displayed by Dash in certain key cases that has given the Continental Detective Agency such a good reputation. His work in protecting the interests of some of the larger shipping companies has been particularly important.'

I began to shift in my seat impatiently.

'But you want to know how this might affect you, correct?'

I smiled awkwardly and nodded.

'The thing for you to understand is that it is not possible for me to expand any particular branch office until that office has reached a certain level of profitability. That level has now been reached by this office.'

Good, I thought, now we'll get to the important part.

'But there is another condition that has to be met before expansion can take place.'

This man, I thought to myself, talks like an inter-office memo!

'And that is just this: suitable talent must be available. We can always find in Rome young men with the required degree of tenacity, enterprise, intelligence and investigative flair. But shipping such young men out to the branch offices in the more remote provinces of the Empire is an expensive business. Besides which, they don't always want to leave Rome. Recruiting locally, on the other hand, has not always been a happy experience for us.'

Get on with it, I thought, get on with it!

'Many of our regional offices are located in areas where the local peoples are just a touch too. . . well, barbarian. . . if I can put it like that, to be of much use

95

as private investigators. They lack the *subtlety* that is an essential characteristic of every good detective. In your case, however, I think we might have solved the problem.'

Great, now we are getting to the good stuff.

'As I told you, Sam, I was most impressed by the account you gave us of your work in Jerusalem. Bearing in mind that it was a situation where you had to act virtually alone, you showed both imagination and tenacity. I take it you are keen on a career in investigation?'

'Absolutely!'

'Good. And how does your father feel about this?'

'Well, he was a private detective himself in his younger days. Before he went into the law, that is,' I said, knowing that I was fudging the truth by suppressing Pop's opposition.

'Good, good. Well what I have in mind is this. If I can be convinced that you have all the qualities it takes to succeed in the service of the Continental Detective Agency then I will offer you a job, starting next calends, at a salary of two thousand denarii paid every calends thereafter.'

A starting salary of twenty-four thousand a year! This would make leaving Law School doubly delightful!

'How does that sound to you, Sam?'

'Great! I mean... it sounds just fine... I mean, I have no problem with that proposition at all. The only thing is...'

'Yes?'

'How do I go about convincing you that I have all of the qualities you're looking for?'

'I was coming to that. Sometime soon—perhaps in the next day or two—Dash and I will have an important case to handle. I want you to come on board just for

96

that case—on full salary of course. And if you prove to be useful, then the job is yours.'

That gave me some qualms. What if Camillus summoned me while I was still helping Pop with the Falcon case? If that happened, I decided, Pop would just have to carry on without me! After all, what Camillus was offering carried long-term career prospects. And that was the hard fact I couldn't ignore.

Camillus and I talked on for some time about the work of the Continental Detective Agency around the known world, and the type of investigative work that would be available for me if I joined the firm.

It sounded fabulous. Just exactly the sort of thing I had always wanted to do.

We talked on until nearly sunset, then Camillus told me he had a dinner appointment, and I left.

In a slow and dreamy fashion I ambled back home, my heart feeling light, and my head full of the wildest possible pictures of my future career.

When I walked into the house, I found Mom and Pop at one end of the kitchen table drinking coffee, while at the other end Naomi was helping Daniel with his home-work. The sound of the twins playing could be heard from the next room.

Should I break the news to them? I wondered.

'Hi, Mom. Hi, Pop. I've got some news for you.'

'Is this news to do with the Continuance Application?' asked Pop.

The Continuance Application! I'd forgotten about that completely! I felt in my jacket pocket. There it was, when it should have been lodged with the clerk of the court half an hour before!

'Oh no!' I moaned.

'What's the problem, Sam?' asked Pop quietly.

For an answer I pulled the document out of my

pocket and showed it to him.

'What happened?' he asked.

'I forgot, Pop. I just forgot. I sort of. . . ' but my excuse ran out of wind before it got any further.

I waited for the blast, but it didn't come. If he had said something, if he had shouted and ranted and raved, I would have felt better. If he had condemned me loud and long for my dereliction of duty I would, of course, have come up with excuses: 'I missed the deadline because. . . ' And after a while I would have believed my own excuses.

But Pop didn't say anything. Which meant that my own conscience condemned me, and no excuse could help me escape from that condemnation.

'I am sorry,' I said lamely, 'I really am.'

The pangs of guilt that were shooting through me were deeply troubling.

'Well. . . I said awkwardly, looking down at my feet and shuffling my shoes, 'what can be done about it?'

'What the failure to lodge that document means,' said Pop quietly, 'is that Paul will have to make a court appearance tomorrow. So I suggest that you hurry to the palace straight away and warn him of that. At least then he will have tonight to prepare.'

'Sure thing,' I said. 'I'll do it immediately.'

'That's always the best time to do anything,' said Pop, so quietly I could barely hear. And then he handed me a folder containing his case-notes for the trial, saying, 'These notes will help Paul prepare his address for tomorrow.'

I hurried out into the street and grabbed a crosstown bus heading towards the palace district. I was glad to be out of the house, so that I didn't have to look at the disappointment in Pop's eyes any longer.

At the palace I was admitted to Paul's guarded

rooms, where I found the great man and his entourage just finishing up their work for the day.

I told Paul about the court appearance he would have to make the next day, and with fumbling apologies told him that it was my fault. Then I gave him the folder that Pop had asked me to pass on.

Titus got out the pen and papyrus he had just packed away, and before long Paul was dictating notes for his address to the court.

Chapter 14

I left them there working—Paul with his eyes closed, head back, and fingertips together as he concentrated, Titus with his head down, writing furiously—while I retreated to a corner to talk to Tim.

'I just feel so rotten,' I said, after I had explained about my failure to keep my solemn promise. 'Paul shouldn't have to go through a court appearance at a time like this, when his life is under threat. And he wouldn't even have to think about another court appearance just now if I had got it right. Can you understand how I feel, Tim?'

'I think I can,' said Tim. 'We all feel guilty at some time or another. And, of course, you *feel* guilty now because you *are* guilty.'

'Oh, that makes me feel a lot better! Thank you very much!'

'Well, when I feel guilty I find that it's better to face it, than to pretend it isn't there.'

'I guess you're right,' I admitted reluctantly. 'Mind you, I really did have another very important engagement that occupied my mind. So, why do I still feel so guilty?'

'It's all mixed up,' said Tim, 'with things like priorities and responsibility to people. Do you know the word "righteousness"?'

'Sounds like religious jargon to me!' I muttered. 'But let's hear your theory about why we are bothered by pangs of guilt.'

'What do you imagine the word "righteousness" means, Sam?' asked Tim.

'Oh, I don't know—being respectable, and upright, and blameless, and very proper, I suppose. Righteous people usually are unbearably smug and self-congratulating I find!' I replied.

'That's what most people think. But "righteous" means being right in all our relationships—especially our relationship with God—and fulfilling the obligations that each relationship imposes. Our relationship to God holds them all together. We all try to run our own lives, our own way, without him. But, when we do we seem to get things out of perspective, get our priorities wrong, we let each other down. We fail to rule ourselves, or society, or the world. All human beings are the same.'

'That's a bit sweeping isn't it?' I protested.

'It is isn't it? But I can remember (because I have copied it out so often) something Paul wrote to the Christians in Rome: "There is no one righteous, not even one; there is no one who understands, no one who seeks God. All have turned away".'

'That makes it sound as though the whole human race is in rebellion against God!'

'Yes it does doesn't it? That's a good word, "rebellion". God is the Maker and Ruler of this world and we are, by nature, in rebellion against him.'

101

'At least we're getting away with it!' I said with a grin.

'Are we?' said Tim returning the grin. 'What about all your guilty feelings? Who started this conversation?'

Before I could answer, one of the Roman guards threw open the door and announced: 'Time, gentlemen, please! All visitors out!'

I quickly seized the opportunity to escape from Tim's theological chit-chat, said goodnight, and departed.

Outside the palace I just missed a bus and decided to walk.

A salty wind was blowing in from the harbour. I turned up my collar, buried my hands in my pockets, and walked briskly.

Leaving the wide public avenues I plunged into suburban streets full of modest middle class villas, and the bungalows of merchants and minor public servants.

Dwelling after dwelling was lit up, each window framing a picture of domestic comfort painted in colours of soft lamplight. I felt very much the outsider; like the one who didn't belong; shut away from the warmth, and the company, and the comfort. A hollowness in the pit of my stomach made me feel like an orphan of the universe.

Making a deliberate effort I shook off the mood, blaming it on Tim's depressing conversation.

At home, Cornelius was in the front sitting room talking to Pop.

'Hello, Sam,' said the old soldier, with his usual grin a mile wide. 'It's a cold night to be out on the streets.'

'I've just walked from the palace,' I explained.

'What a pity,' said the commander, 'I've just driven from there. If I'd known you were about I could have given you a lift. We must have missed each other on the road.'

'Cornelius has arranged those interviews with palace staff that you and I have to conduct tomorrow, Sam,' said Pop.

I was relieved to hear that. I had been a little worried that, after I forgot to lodge the document, Pop might exclude me from the investigation.

'This is the list of the new servants employed in the last four weeks,' said Cornelius. 'There are exactly six—three men and three women.'

'I suppose we needn't bother about the women, Pop,' I said.

'Why not? We keep refering to the Falcon as a male, but we don't know that to be the case—no one does.'

'So the Falcon could be a woman?'

'Why not? None of the Falcon's murders, that we know of, has required extraordinary physical strength.'

'And many of them have been poisonings,' I added. 'And poison is a woman's weapon.'

'It is certainly true that arsenic trioxide can be handled equally well by persons of either gender,' said Pop.

'So you'll interview all six of these people tomorrow?' asked the commander.

'You may be assured that we will, Cornelius my dear brother,' said Pop.

'Well, you take the list. You'll notice that I've marked a time against each name, but it's a suggested time only—it's when they would be easily available in the normal round of their chores. Now, tell me the latest on the case—bring me up to date.'

So Pop told Cornelius about all of our investigations,

discoveries, and conclusions thus far. I left them to their talk, and went into the kitchen, where I found my supper being kept warm in the oven.

My sleep that night was plagued with nightmares in which I was trapped in a huge courtroom. The vast, echoing court was furnished with giant, over-sized fittings that towered high above me. The judicial bench was so tall that I couldn't see the judge's face, only hear his voice, pronouncing me guilty over and over again: 'You are found guilty, Sam Bartholomew,' boomed the voice. 'Unjust, unjust, unjust.'

The unseen judge pressed a button that rang a bell to summon the guards who would drag me away to the condemned cell.

I woke up in a cold sweat, in the grey light of dawn. And the bell from my nightmare was still ringing. Slowly surfacing, I realised it was the telephone.

I hurried downstairs before the phone woke the whole house. But Pop had beaten me to it. When I got there, he was muttering acknowledgements into the phone and scribbling on a writing pad at the same time.

Hanging up the phone he turned to me and said, 'An interesting development, Sam. Our friend Mr Cairo was murdered last night.'

Chapter 15

Pop and I sat at the kitchen table warming ourselves with hot coffee as he filled me in on the call.

'It was Cornelius who rang with the news. Apparently the city watch discovered the body an hour ago, and it is standard procedure for them to ring the commander. And, because of our conversation last night, he thought we might like to know.'

'Are we going to have a look at the scene of the crime?' I asked.

'We are. As soon as we have finished our coffee and pulled on some clothes. I've made a note of the address, and I think that if we add our investigations to those of the city watch, we may learn something to our advantage.'

Even early in the morning, when he was only half awake, Pop still talked like a lawyer!

We travelled by cab through the dawn light with the sun sitting on the eastern hills, like a rich ripe orange in a bowl. The light it cast had the pale unreality of stage lighting, making the outlines of the buildings very sharp and clear, and the bands of shadow blacker than ink.

Mr Cairo's body had been found in the narrow alley that ran along the back wall of the *Rigor Mortis*. Here, amongst the empty wine barrels, almost directly below the window of his own office, lay the crumpled heap of clothing that was once Cairo.

Pop and I stood on the edge of the small group of city watch officers as the location of the corpse was marked with chalk and photographs were taken.

We introduced ourselves to Captain Rufus Metellus, who was in charge of the case.

'Pleased to meet you,' he responded. 'When I telephoned Commander Cornelius he warned me that you might show up.'

'Can we move the body now, Captain?' asked one of his men.

'Has the medical examiner finished?'

'All done, sir.'

'Then tell the mortuary people they can have the corpse,' said Metellus.

'When was the body found?' asked Pop.

'About an hour before dawn,' replied the Captain. 'Two of my officers on regular foot patrol came across it.'

'How long had it been there?'

'Less than two hours. That's when the foot patrol passes this spot—on a two-hourly cycle. But from the lack of blood on the cobblestones I'd say he didn't die here. He was killed somewhere else and his body dumped here.'

'In between city watch patrols?'

'Exactly.'

At that point, the medical examiner joined our group, and Captain Metellus introduced us. 'This is

Dr Neronius Nausea—he'll be in charge of the autopsy.'

'What was the cause of death?' I asked.

'A Roman short sword,' replied the doctor, 'expertly inserted under the ribs in an upward thrusting motion. A classical stroke really—you can see it being practised any day of the week at any military academy around the Empire.'

'Are you saying doctor, that the blow was struck by someone with military training?' asked Pop.

'Possibly—but not necessarily.'

'Isn't that just a typical medical answer!' growled Captain Metellus.

'I'm trying to be realistic,' said Dr Nausea defensively. 'Almost any child who has ever played at soldiers has practised the upward thrust with the short sword under the ribs and into the heart.'

'Would it have required much strength?' I asked, 'Could a woman have struck the blow?'

'Those effete, feeble, fainting noblewomen could not, but a reasonably muscular servant woman could have.'

'And when did he die?' asked Pop.

'I won't know for sure until I perform the autopsy. And even then I may not know for sure unless I can find out when he ate his last meal.'

'Have a guess for us,' insisted Captain Metellus.

'As a guess—late last night. Somewhere in the vicinity of midnight perhaps.'

'Which confirms that he was not killed here,' said Metellus. 'Thanks for your help doctor.'

Dr Nausea took his leave from us, climbed aboard the waiting mortuary van, and was gone.

'The next thing,' said Metellus, rubbing his chin in a thoughtful manner, 'is to find out where this Cairo guy did actually get his chest full of bronze.'

'Have you checked his office?' asked Pop.

'I don't even know where his office is,' replied the Captain.

'Immediately above our heads,' said Pop.

'Well—what are we waiting for then? Let's have a look.'

The street door was standing open, revealing the steep, narrow staircase behind it. At the top of the stairs Cairo's office door was locked.

It was a timber door with a frosted glass panel on which was gold lettering that read:

Cairo Incorporated
Business Consultant
and
Commission Agent

'Just a long winded way of saying "crook", I suspect,' said Captain Metellus when he saw the sign.

'And your suspicions would be entirely correct,' said Pop.

When the door refused to respond to a little gentle pressure, Metellus used his night stick to smash the glass. Then he reached inside, unlatched the door, and pushed it open.

We stepped over the fragments of glass into an office that was dramatically changed since our visit of the previous afternoon.

Then the office had been overcrowded with bundles of paper on shelves, filing cabinets, and every inch of desk space. But it had been neatly overcrowded. Now it was a shambles.

'Someone has searched this office,' said Metellus.

'And they have searched it very thoroughly,' added Pop, 'having first murdered its occupant.'

As he spoke Pop pointed to the pool of blackened, dried blood that had soaked into the carpet behind the desk.

'This looks like where he was killed all right,' I said. 'And then, while Mr Cairo quietly bled to death, his killer searched the files.'

'A cold blooded swine,' murmured Metellus. 'But what was he looking for?'

'While I cannot be one hundred percent certain,' said Pop, 'I have some ideas on that subject. Furthermore I believe the murderer found what he was looking for.'

Pop picked up the waste paper basket and showed us the ashes of burned papers that lay at the bottom of the container.

'He found what he was looking for—and destroyed it,' I said.

'Precisely,' said Pop.

'Fill me in,' said Captain Metellus. 'What's your theory?'

Pop filled him in—explaining the possible role of Mr Cairo in assisting the Falcon to gain access to the palace.

'But how could that have led to his death?' asked Metellus, after Pop had finished explaining.

'I speculate that when Sam and I spoke to Mr Cairo yesterday afternoon his first thought was how to make money out of the information in his possession,' said Pop.

'But that was easy!' I protested. 'Selling us the information would have turned a handsome profit for him—especially at the prices he was quoting.'

'True,' said Pop, 'but does it not occur to you that the late Egyptian gentlemen may have seen even bigger profits in *not* supplying us with the information?'

'I don't follow.'

'It may have occurred to Mr Cairo that the maximum profit was to be had from blackmailing the Falcon.'

'Then he did know who the Falcon is?'

'He certainly knew who had come to him asking for help in obtaining access to the palace. Our information told him that this was a Falcon operation. He would have concluded that the man with whom he dealt was either the Falcon himself, or else the Falcon's agent. And knowing the underworld gossip about the reluctance of the Falcon to use agents, he would have assumed the man to be the Falcon .'

'That's a dangerous position to be in—knowing the identity of the Falcon. Cairo would have been about the only man in the Empire to know that!'

'Indeed. Which is why the Falcon could not afford to let him live.'

'So—it was the Falcon who did all this?' said Metellus, waving his arm in a broad gesture over the chaotic office.

'Indeed,' said Pop. 'He needed to be sure that Cairo had made no record of their transaction that could have implicated him.'

'So, by setting up a meeting with this man, Cairo was signing his own death warrant?' I said.

'Quite correct,' said Pop, 'Mr Cairo would have, naturally, taken some precautions to protect his own personal safety. Perhaps he was carrying a weapon. But against a deadly assassin such as the Falcon, Cairo's precautions were futile.'

'And the corpse now lying in the morgue is the result,' growled Metellus. 'So—what can be done about it? I don't fancy my chances of tracking down the Falcon when all the top authorities in the Empire have tried and failed. What do you suggest, Mr

Bartholomew?'

'I suggest that Sam and I continue our investigation. Very slowly, inch by inch, we are closing in on the Falcon. Persistence must be our watch-word. Solomon says: "Hard work gives a man power". We will continue to work hard, and if our work unearths the falcon, then you, Captain, will have your murderer.'

'You'd better be careful, Mr Bartholomew,' said Metellus.'

'At this very moment I can feel the chill of the Falcon's breath. I assure you Captain, that Sam and I will be very careful indeed.'

Later, in the street outside Cairo's office, I asked Pop about our plans.

'Home for a hot breakfast first, I think,' he said, 'and then to the palace to interview those half dozen servants who are recent arrivals.'

'Could one of them actually be the Falcon, Pop?'

'Quite possibly. So, in the next few hours we could be face to face with the Falcon—without even knowing it.'

Chapter 16

The list of new servants supplied by Commander Cornelius contained six names. Three women—Cassandra, Vashti, and Naissa; and three men—Shallum, Petronius and Theopoulos. The plan was that Pop would ask the questions, and I would take notes during the interviews.

The first of these servants we caught up with was Cassandra—a Greek woman, very short, thin and wiry, nearer to sixty than fifty, and with a permanently sour expression on her face.

We found her in a pantry just off the main palace kitchen. Pop introduced himself as a lawyer acting on the authority of Commander Cornelius, and asked for a few minutes of her time.

She made it quite clear that she regarded us as a plain nuisance, and that she was only agreeing to talk to us as a way of getting rid of us.

'Now, Cassandra,' said Pop, 'you've been here at the palace for how long?'

'Two weeks. Two long and miserable weeks.'

'Why so miserable?'

'Because I have never worked in such a badly organised place in my life before. Perhaps I'm getting old, but it seems to me that no one cares about standards any more. Look at these young servants: their clothes are sloppy, their manners are sloppy. What sort of parents let them grow up like this?'

'If you find this place so uncongenial, why are you working here?'

'I've got to work somewhere haven't I?'

'Where were you working last?'

'Up the coast at Ptolemais. In a private house. The home of a wealthy trader.'

'Why did you leave?'

'He went bankrupt. We all left. I warned the other servants that the master was going bankrupt. I warned them. But they didn't listen to me. And then it happened. And we were all out of work.'

'How did you get the job here?'

'I knocked on the kitchen door one morning, spoke to the under-butler, a man named Factotum, and it so happened they needed an extra person so here I am.'

'What exactly is your job?'

'I'm a cup-bearer under the direction of the cellar master.'

'Do you intend to stay?'

'Whadda ya mean?'

'Since you say you are unhappy here, are you intending to stay?'

'Being unhappy is no reason to leave! When have I ever been happy in a job? Never! That's when! And you know why? Because nobody ever listens to me, that's why. Like last night for instance, they were decanting some red wine in the kitchen for the evening banquet upstairs. And I said to them, don't decant that wine too soon, too much air is bad for it, it will not be at its best, I said. But did they listen to me? No, they did not! And the result? The wine was sent back as undrinkable and a new bottle sent for. But still they don't listen.'

This woman, I decided, was the world's number one, grade A sourpuss.

'Have you been a domestic servant for the whole of your life?' asked Pop.

'Of course I have! What else is there for an unmarriageable freeborn woman to do?'

'Why unmarriageable?'

'You certainly ask personal questions, don't you? All right, I'll tell you: because of this ugly mug, that's why. I never had beauty, and my father never had the money for a big dowry, so I never got married, get it?'

As she was snarling out her answer I thought to myself that it was more a case of an ugly personality than an ugly face.

'And whereabouts have you spent this lifetime in domestic service?' asked Pop.

'In many places. Many, many places. Some places that would surprise you. I had a very senior position with one of the great noble families in Rome. I was with them for many years.'

'And why are you not still with them?'

'They lost their money in foolish investments. You know what those idiots did? They invested their money in vineyards in Britannicus! Can you imagine those woad-wearing barbarians of Britons knowing how to tend vineyards? Anyway, how can you grow grapes for wines in a place that has seventeen different types of rain and no proper sunshine? It was a real dumb investment. I told them that. But they wouldn't listen to me. And I was right. And now that family is broke. And I have to look for work wherever I can find it.'

114

'Just one other question. . . '

'No! No other questions. I've wasted enough of my time today with your fool questions. Now I'm going back to work.' With that she stomped out of the pantry slamming the door behind her.

'I feel sorry for someone who is so bitter at life,' said Pop. 'At the same time—I'm glad she doesn't work for us!'

Next on the list was a young Egyptian woman named Vashti.

We found her in the palace scullery, half-heartedly scrubbing her way through a vast pile of dirty pots and pans. Her carelessness and minimum effort seemed to be proof of the complaint that Cassandra had made about the younger generation of domestic servants.

Vashti was only too happy to stop work, and made it clear she would talk to us for as long as we wished. Anything was preferable to work!

'What exactly is your job, Vashti?' began Pop.

'I am what you call the body of the dog,' she replied.

'The dog's body?'

'That is what I said. I have to do everything and anything. Sometimes I am up in the big banquet room serving on the tables and hearing the musicians play and having a wonderful time. And sometimes I am down here scrubbing, scrubbing, scrubbing on filthy pots and pans!'

'So you are a maid of all work?'

'All work is right. I do all the work because the others are so lazy!'

'You have been here for how long?'

'I don't know. Sometimes when I am doing jobs like this it feels like years and years.'

'Well, I happen to know it is more like weeks than years.'

115

'If you know, then why you ask?'

'Because I would like to have a more precise figure: how long have you been at the palace?'

'Vashti not sure,' she said sullenly.

'You must have some idea.'

'Why should Vashti try to keep track of time in this place?'

'Well, if you can't help us. . . ' said Pop, pretending he was about to break off the interview.

'I remember! I try hard and remember! One moment and I remember!' cried Vashti in alarm at the prospect of returning to the pots and pans.

'Ah yes,' she said, 'it is coming back to me now. It is three weeks. That is how long I have been here. It just feels like much, much more than three weeks.'

'How did you get the job here?'

'My last master had a gambling debt, and to pay the debt he sold my employment contract to the under-butler, that awful man Factotum.'

'How come an Egyptian girl like you is working here, in a Roman city, in the province of Judaea?'

'In Egypt we have good years and we have bad years. It all depends on the flood. My father, he is a boatman on the Nile, and so are my brothers. But we also have a little farm. Without the farm there is not enough to eat. If some year the flood doesn't come—someone have to leave home. One less mouth to feed.'

'And you left home in a bad year?'

'That's right. First I get a job in the house of the harbour master at Joppa. Then a man named Impertinax comes to visit. He sees me. He likes what he sees. And he offers me a job in his house in Caesarea.'

'Why did he do that?'

'Look at me! I don't look so bad, eh? His wife, she

look bad. . . old and ugly. So Impertinax he hires me. In the mornings I do a little light work in the kitchen, and then in the afternoons he and I. . . '

'I think we get the picture,' said Pop hastily.

'And then that swine—he sell me to pay a gambling debt! If I could get my hands on his throat I would strangle him. And I would laugh while I do it!'

These last words were uttered in so violent a fashion, that I began to regard this Egyptian as a dangerous young woman.

'If you meet my old master Impertinax,' snarled Vashti, banging one of the iron pots for emphasis as she spoke, 'I ask that you spit in his face for me! That filthy swine! I don't believe there was a gambling debt! I think he got a pretty new kitchenmaid and was tired of Vashti! Swine that he is!'

'Thank you for your time, Vashti,' said Pop, and then turning to me he added, 'I think we have accomplished all we can here for the time being.'

So we left the young Egyptian lady to have her temper tantrum in the privacy of the scullery, while we moved on elsewhere.

'What did you make of her, Pop?' I asked, once we were out of earshot. 'Was she telling the truth, or was she not?'

'Always a difficult question to answer, Sam. Her story of how she came to be employed here at the palace may be perfectly true. Or it may be the cover story the Falcon has invented for her.'

'Or, as unlikely as it seems, she may be the Falcon herself. Or Cassandra may be.'

'Indeed, it may be the case that the whole persona presented by each of those women is a false one, designed to hide a deadly purpose.'

'Which makes it all very confusing,' I complained.

'So—where to next?'

'To talk to the first of the men on the list, Shallum. An interesting case because he is—according to Cornelius's notes—a Jew in the service of the Romans. Or, at least, that is what he appears to be.'

Chapter 17

We found Shallum in the palace bakery, and had to wait until he had finished pounding and kneading a large lump of bread dough before he could speak to us.

Having placed the mound of dough on a window-sill in the sun he turned to us and said, 'I can talk to you now gentlemen, while the dough is rising.'

Pop again explained who we were, and our authority for asking questions. 'To begin with Shallum, how long have you been employed here at the palace?'

'A couple of weeks,' he replied.

'And how did you come by the job?'

'To tell you the truth, I was in search of better pay. I move around a lot, to be honest. Been bitten by the travel bug. So I like to see different places. And, like I say, I'm always in search of the perfect pay packet.'

'How long have you been a—what shall I call it—a compulsive traveller?'

'All my life. My father was a sea captain, a master mariner. Every few years he would shift home ports.

So the whole family would pack up and move.'

'So, where have you lived then?'

'You name it, I've lived there. I was born in Alexandria, for instance. . . '

'Not in Judaea?'

'Why would you ask that? Oh, because I'm a Jew you mean? Well, I'm a Jew of the "dispersion" as we're called—not a Judaean Jew.'

'And you were born in Alexandria?'

'Correct. But we left there when I was only four. In fact, I couldn't remember the place, and when I lived there a few years ago, it was like discovering it for the first time.'

'Have you ever lived in Rome itself?'

'More than once. When I get tired of drifting and want to settle down for a while it is usually Rome that I head for.'

'Do you always work as a cook, wherever you travel?'

'Not just as a cook—as a pastry cook. I am a very good pastry cook, and I can always find a demand for my services.'

'Do you, as a Jew, find no difficulty in working in gentile households?'

'Well. . . to be absolutely honest. . . my mother was a good Jewish mother, but not very religious, if you take my meaning. And my father. . . well, my father he was a seaman, and like a lot of seamen he was pretty wild.'

Shallum turned away from us for a moment to take a look at the lump of bread dough on the window-sill. His age was hard to pick. He had a head of thick black hair, without a trace of grey, but his face was lined and weathered. Probably around early middle age I would have guessed, but it would have been a very rough guess.

'Anything else you want to know?' he asked.

'Who employed you here at the palace?' asked Pop.

'The under-butler—Factotum. He employs all the kitchen staff.'

'Did you have a job lined up when you arrived in Caesarea?'

'No, I never plan my movements too far in advance. I just roll up and take my chances. But I am well known in some of the best circles for my pastries, and I carry excellent references with me—so, like I say, I can always get good paying work.'

'Then why did you come to Caesarea? That is to say, why Caesarea rather than some other city?'

'Because I had never been here before. And my feet were getting itchy. No better reason than that.'

'Are you a married man, Mr Shallum?'

'No. You can't have a wife and family when you move around as much as I do. A girl in every port, that's my style.'

Our remaining questions went back over territory already covered, and after a few more minutes we took our leave from the wandering Jewish pastrycook.

'What did you make of his story, Sam?' asked Pop, as we walked away.

'Well, it strikes me, Pop. . .'

'Don't call me Pop!'

'. . . that this man has the perfect cover story for the Falcon. If he really is the man we are looking for his erratic movements around the Empire, his "travel bug" as he calls it, could cover his movements from one murder to the next.'

'Indeed it could.'

'And!' I went on, becoming quite excited, 'And his job would be just perfect for a poisoner! Who better to feed victims arsenic trioxide than someone who is cooking for them?'

'Who indeed?' said Pop, 'However, I have my doubts. If anything, the perfect match between Shallum's cover story and the Falcon's movements—and murders—make me suspect that Shallum could not possibly be the Falcon. After all, would the Falcon be so open in admitting how widely he travels? And would he invite suspicion by using poison as a murder weapon when he himself is handling food?'

'I see what you mean. But, what about this: what if the Falcon covers his tracks by being so far out in the open that no one suspects him?'

'A double-bluff in fact?' said Pop thoughtfully. 'It could be, Sam, it certainly could be.'

And we moved on to our next interview.

This was with a young maid named Naissa, a local girl. We found her in one of the palace's many dining rooms, setting a table for lunch.

She agreed to answer our questions, but she seemed rather intimidated and frightened by our approach.

'Now, tell me Naissa, how long have you worked here at the palace?' asked Pop.

'A week and a half, sir,' she replied.

'And how did you get the job here?'

'My mum got me the job, sir. Her Uncle Eli, that's my Great Uncle Eli, used to work here, sir. And he gave my mum a note to bring along to Mr Factotum, and he said he would try me out to see if I could do the work, but that he couldn't promise anything permanent. Not until he'd given me a one month trial, sir.'

'And how's it working out so far?'

To our astonishment, and embarrassment, the young woman burst into tears at this point.

'Here, take my handkerchief and dry your eyes Naissa,' said Pop gently. 'You mustn't get so upset. Now, what is the problem?'

'It's the fish knives, sir,' she sniffled, 'I always puts the fish knives in the wrong place and then Mr Factotum comes along and ticks me off, but I still keep forgetting.'

And she burst out howling again. I put an arm around her shoulders to comfort her, and she responded by burying her face in my shoulder and sobbing solidly for several minutes. I found this rather embarrassing, but at the same time I couldn't help noticing what a cute little thing she was.

Eventually the tears dried up and Naissa detached herself from my now very damp shoulder.

'Have you been sent by Mr Factotum, sir?' she asked Pop miserably, 'to see if I'm doing my work?'

'No, no, not at all,' said Pop. 'As I explained at the beginning, we are making enquiries under the authority of Commander Cornelius. It's a matter of palace security, nothing to do with your work. Now, if you pull yourself together and answer our questions, Sam here will give you a hand with your table settings and make sure that everything is correct.'

'Oh, will you, sir?' she said, turning to me, with her big brown eyes looking as soft as a doe. Well, I had to say yes, didn't I?

'Now, Naissa,' said Pop, returning to the interview, 'you've been here a week and a half?'

'Yes, sir.'

'Where else have you worked before the palace?'

'At my Uncle Abe's coffee shop, down on the Forum, sir.'

Then it struck me. Of course I'd seen this girl before. She was not a very good waitress, as I recalled. She was the one who was inclined to spill the coffee and get the bill wrong.

'Why did you give up that job to come here?'

'Well. . . no particular reason. . . sir.'

'You just wanted a change?'

'I suppose so, sir.'

'And what do your tasks here entail?'

'Beg pardon?'

'What do you do?'

'Oh. I set the tables for each meal. In the middle of the morning I do the lunch tables, and in the middle of the afternoon I do the dinner tables. And during the meals I help to serve.'

'Who supervises the food service?'

'Mr Factotum is in charge, sir. Wherever the governor is dining he is there in person, supervising us maids doing the serving. In the other dining rooms, one of the senior maids is in charge.'

'I see.'

'Can I go now please, sir? I have two other tables to do after this one, and I don't want Mr Factotum to be upset with me again.' She started to sob again, but, pulling a tiny lace handkerchief out of a pocket, stifled the sob.

'Yes, of course. Thank you for being so helpful, Naissa,' said Pop. 'Sam—may I see your notes please?'

I handed Pop the notebook in which were recorded the interviews we had done so far, and he sat down in a corner of the room to study the notes while I helped Naissa.

In fact, she had done the job quite well. Her problem, I decided was just a lack of confidence that made her flustered and unsure. I told her so. And I patted her arm and said encouraging things, and she smiled at me in the sweetest possible way. But eventually she had to leave to set other tables, while I returned to the hunt for the Falcon.

'What is your summing up of young Naissa?' asked Pop.

'An innocent abroad,' I said.

'Literally innocent?'

'Literally! Well, she certainly isn't the Falcon—is she?' I said belligerently.

'Quite correct. The Falcon has been operating longer than she has been out of school.'

'Well, there you are then.'

'However, she could be an agent of the Falcon.'

'Nonsense! You can see by looking at her that there's not a criminal thought inside that pretty little head.'

'Yes, she is very pretty,' said Pop, making a totally irrelevant remark. 'Nonetheless, she could be an innocent tool in the hands of a master criminal.'

'He wouldn't dare!'

'Who wouldn't?'

'The Falcon!'

'I think the point is, Sam, that he would dare. That is how the Falcon operates: in a most daring and unpredictable manner.'

'Hhhmmm!' I snorted, in the most skeptical manner I could manage. 'Let's move on to the next interview. Who is it?'

'A man named Theopoulos, who has the highly relevant task of being the governor's official Taster.'

Chapter 18

To locate Theopoulos we had to go to the governor's quarters, on the top floor of the eastern wing of the palace. From here every room had a magnificent sweeping view of the ocean.

We found Theopoulos in a kind of ante-chamber, where a number of the governor's personal staff sat waiting to be summoned into the presence of His Excellency, to perform whatever their particular function might be.

Once more Pop explained that we were lawyers interviewing staff, under the authority of Commander Cornelius, on a matter of palace security. Theopoulos, a sandy-haired, freckle-faced man in his early thirties appeared to be quite happy to co-operate.

'How long have you been on the palace staff, Mr Theopoulos?' asked Pop.

'A bit over three weeks,' he replied.

'How did you come to join the staff?'

'I volunteered.'

'Volunteered?'

'Yes. As you can understand, it is hard for His Excellency to find someone to fill the post of official taster.'

'Because it's dangerous?'

'Yes.'

'Just exactly what do you do?' asked Pop.

'I taste a small sample of everything that is served to His Excellency to either eat or drink. If I die, then the food, or drink, has been poisoned. I'm the safety system.'

'You are happy to risk being poisoned?'

'Yes.'

'And you volunteered for this job?'

'I did.'

'Strange behaviour, Mr Theopoulos. Why did you do it?'

'I felt it was the least I could do in return for what His Excellency did for my family.'

'Tell me about it.'

'Two years ago there was an uprising in some parts of the province against Roman rule. The leader of the uprising was a messianic pretender.'

'A man of Egyptian birth—yes, I remember.'

'His Excellency crushed the rebellion, but the Egyptian escaped. In the two years since then, His Excellency has ordered a continuing search for this rebel leader who remains in hiding. Some of the forays in search of this man he has led in person.'

'Indeed, some of the most bloodthirsty and merciless,' said Pop, lowering his voice, 'were the raids he led himself. He regarded them as sport—as hunting parties.'

This comment seemed to make Theopoulos uncomfortable, but he cleared his throat and continued, 'Anyway, some six months ago one of these raids went down the coast, as far as Joppa. And that's where my family live, in a little village just north of Joppa. When the soldiers rode up, with His Excellency at the head dressed in full Roman military uniform, we were all very frightened.'

'You were living at home with your family at the time?'

'I was. We were all fishermen, my brothers and I. Ours is a coastal village and all the families live off the sea. On the day when His Excellency and his soldiers arrived we were, as I said, very frightened.'

'Given the reputation of His Excellency,' muttered Pop quietly, 'I can well understand that.'

Once again, Theopoulos looked distinctly uncomfortable.

'One of the sergeants,' he continued, 'pointed to my three brothers and me and said: "Any one of these might be that Egyptian trouble-maker. Let's kill them all". You must understand that having a Greek father and a Jewish mother gives us an appearance that could be mistaken for Egyptian. I explained that to the sergeant. But he turned to his men and said: "Let's kill them anyway—to be on the safe side". And I thought we were all going to die.'

Theopoulos stopped and swallowed hard, and then continued, 'I pleaded with the leader of the soldiers— the man wearing the most splendid uniform—to spare our lives. I did not know at the time that it was His Excellency. I swore that if he spared our lives I would find a way to serve him with my life. The other soldiers had drawn their swords, and our lives hung in the balance. The leader seemed to consider my plea for several moments, then he turned to his sergeant and said "Spare them. Ride on!", and a moment later they were all gone and we were still alive.'

'You were most fortunate. Providence was gracious to you and your family that day,' commented Pop.

'When I understood that it was His Excellency who had, in person, spared our lives, I felt I had to honour my solemn oath and find a way to serve him with my life. For many months I looked for an opportunity to do so. When I read in the *Caesarea Daily* that His Excellency needed a personal taster, I saw that my opportunity had arisen, so I presented myself at the palace and offered my services.'

'But as taster to the governor you might *die!*' I interrupted. 'Haven't you thought of that?'

'Of course I have. But if I die now my aged mother and my young sister will still have my three brothers to support them. If we had been killed that day—as we so nearly were—they would have had no one. My father, you see, has been dead for many years. It is for sparing my family that I must serve His Excellency with my life.'

'But the governor is not,' I whispered, lowering my voice, 'a good man. Everyone says that he exercises the powers of a king with the disposition of a slave. He is said to be utterly merciless. He probably only spared you and your brothers that day because he was bored.'

'Even if all you say is true,' said Theopoulos, 'it does not change my solemn oath. If His Excellency is a bad man, then I am prepared to die for a bad man, if that is how I can serve him.'

'Does Governor Felix realise,' asked Pop, 'how fortunate he is to have you as his official taster?'

'It does not matter if he realises or not,' replied Theopoulos. 'That is the path to which I am committed.'

As Pop and I walked down the wide, marbled corridor that led from the governor's luxurious apartments, I shook my head in disbelief, 'What do you make of that story, Pop?' I asked.

'It may be perfectly true,' said Pop, 'The truth is very often stranger than the wildest imagination. Or it may be that we have just spoken face to face with the Falcon.'

'Really? Could Theopoulos be. . . ?'

'He could. Almost anyone could be the Falcon, so little is known of that secretive assassin. And imagine the situation for yourself. The Falcon arrives in Caesarea, sees that paragraph in the *Daily* about Felix needing a personal taster, so he volunteers with an elaborate story to back up his extraordinary offer of service.'

'Yes! I see what you mean! Who could be better placed to poison someone, than a person on the governor's staff we all think is there to deter poisoners! Brilliant!'

'But I warn you, Sam. Such thoughts may be pure speculation, and Theopoulos may be exactly what he claims to be.'

Our last interview was with a middle-aged Roman named Petronius. A former slave and now a freedman, he was employed as assistant cellar master.

There being no true cellars, or dungeons, in Herod's palace, we found Mr Petronius in a dank, dark room at the back of the building, that served as the wine cellars.

He was a short, portly, bald-headed man with a cheerful countenance, sparkling eyes, and the sort of red nose that suggested too much sampling of his own wares.

'Oh yes, I'm quite happy to help, quite happy,' he burbled, when we explained our mission. 'Fire away, ask any questions you like, anything you like at all.'

130

'How long have you been here?' asked Pop, beginning with his standard opening.

'Here? Well, let me see now. Since about ten o'clock I should think, ten o'clock this morning that is,' he replied, adding with a foolish giggle. 'I didn't sleep here, you understand.'

'What I mean is—how long have you been on the palace staff?'

'Oh, is that what you want to know. Well, you should have said. Or I should have understood. I do get muddled you know. Now, what did you want to know?'

'How long have you been on the palace staff!'

'Oh, yes, of course! That's what you wanted to know, isn't it! Well, I'd say two weeks. Yes, that would be about it. Two weeks. Or possibly three. On second thoughts it could have been three. But no longer than three, I'm certain of that. Does that help?'

'It does. Second question: how did you get your job here?'

'How did I get it? Well, old Factotum appointed me, that's how.'

'Yes, I understand that Factotum appoints the staff, but what I want to know is how he came to appoint you.'

'Oh, right. I see your point. Well, I was here, in Caesarea don't you know, and I rather didn't want to go to sea again. Most unpleasant I'd found the voyage. It didn't stay still. The deck that is. It moved up and down all the time, up and down, up and down. I start to feel ill just thinking about it.'

'You'd better take a seat, Mr Petronius.'

'Yes I think I will. Up and down, up and down. Just thinking about it does awful things to a fellah's stomach. Perhaps I should take a small glass of wine—for my

131

stomach's sake, don't ya know.'

'In a moment. Answer a few more questions first.'

'If you insist.'

'I do! If you dislike ocean travel so much, how did you come to be on a ship in the first place?'

'I'd signed on, hadn't I? As quartermaster. I was in charge of the stores and the supplies and things.'

'You signed on a ship as quartermaster? When you can't stand sea voyages?'

'Well, I didn't know that at the time, did I? I mean to say, I'd spent my entire life ashore. And a very boring life it had been. So I thought that before I died I should travel a bit, see the world, don't ya know?'

'So you signed on as quartermaster?'

'Now you've got the picture! Yes, that's exactly what I did. Terrible mistake it turned out to be. I mean to say, the Mediterranean looks so calm and placid most of the time. When you're looking at it from the shore that is. But out there in the middle, well that's another story altogether. It quite took me by surprise. Most unpleasant surprise indeed.'

'And what did you do about your "unpleasant surprise"?'

'I got off, that's what I did. First civilised Roman city I came to, I got off. And it was Caesarea. We touched at a few barbarous places in Cyprus and Syria on the way, but I didn't like the look of those. But I could see at once this was a proper Roman city. A place where a man could live in some comfort. So I signed myself off that wretched ship and came looking for work.'

'And ended up here as assistant cellar master?'

'Precisely. The job's a bit below what I'm used to of course, but then again it's a case of "any port in a storm". I say, that's not bad is it? Any port in a storm! That's jolly good that is.'

132

And so we left Mr Petronius, looking like a chubby pink gnome, chuckling away to himself as he reached for a bottle of wine—to be taken 'for his stomach's sake' no doubt!

Chapter 19

'Could *that* have been the Falcon?' I asked Pop as we walked back towards the main part of the palace building.

'Why not?' was Pop's reply. 'What better disguise than a dithering fool to hide a sharp and evil mind? And his story is one that cannot be checked. Only his stomach knows if his story is true.'

'And as assistant cellar master he could easily poison the wine,' I added. 'The problem with this case is that we have too many suspects.'

'Truly, too many false paths lure our attention,' said Pop, ' and we must eliminate blind alleys.

It was now lunch time, and we left the palace precincts to lunch at the restaurant across the road known as *Herod's Leftovers*. It was named after Herod the Great, who had built both the city of Caesarea and the palace which still bore his name long after his death. Since Herod had been a wealthy gourmandising tyrant the expression 'Herod's leftovers' had come to mean an excellent meal. And that's what we got at the restaurant—an excellent lunch.

As we finished our meal I asked, 'How do we go about eliminating the dross from this case? How do we decide which leads to follow and which to abandon?'

'Let me turn the question back to you, Sam. Which of the six we interviewed this morning would you eliminate?'

'Naissa, obviously.'

'I suspected you would say that. But of the others—who is now crossed off your list?'

'Well. . . perhaps. . . none of them, I guess.'

'How so?'

'Well—apart from Naissa—any of the other five could either be the Falcon, or an agent of the Falcon. For this assassin to be as invisible as he or she has been for so long, he or she must not look like a murderer.'

'Quite correct. And I would return the name of Naissa to the list. She alone of the six could not be the Falcon, but she could be an unwitting pawn in the hands of that bird of prey.'

'On that analysis we can eliminate no one!' I complained.

'We must go on gathering facts, we must increase our knowledge. As our knowledge of this case grows, and we evaluate what we learn, we will shorten that list of suspects. Solomon says: "Just as honey is sweet on the tongue, knowledge and wisdom are good for the soul". We keep investigating, Sam, and we stay alert.'

'So where do we go to now?'

'Shortly Paul is due to make his appearance in court. . . ' I blushed with embarrassment as I remembered my failure of the previous evening. '. . . and we must be there as his legal advisers. But before the afternoon court session begins, we have time to pay a short call on a certain under-butler.'

We found Factotum in a small pantry that opened off the main kitchen. He was in his shirt sleeves finishing off a large lunch with a generous glass of port.

'I do apologise for disturbing your meal,' said Pop in his most diplomatic manner.

'How may I be of service to you, sir?' replied the starchy butler, staring down his long nose with a lofty glare that would fry eggs in a freezer.

'My name is Ben Bartholomew. I am a lawyer investigating a matter of palace security. I have the authority of Commander Cornelius to do so. Please take a look at this list of names, Mr Factotum. The commander drew up this list for me, as people who had been employed at the palace in the last four weeks. Do you recognise them?'

Factotum balanced a pair of gold-rimmed glasses on the end of his monumental proboscis and murmured, 'Yes... yes... I recognise them all. I hired them. Hiring and firing is my responsibility, sir.'

That final 'sir' seemed to emerge from the butler in a most reluctant manner, like a drunk being ejected from a bar at closing time.

'And what can you tell me about them?' persisted Pop.

'Well, there's a Roman, a Greek, a Jew, two Egyptian women and a local girl. What else is there to say... sir?'

'Were there any unusual circumstances surrounding the hiring of any of the six? For example—did you hire any of them as a favour to a friend? Were you especially requested to hire any of them?'

'Certainly not! The hiring practices of this palace are strictly impartial. Staff are hired on merit only, and only when appropriate vacancies occur. Furthermore,

136

young and untried staff are hired for a probationary period. And for experienced staff I always require references. Does that adequately answer your question... sir?'

'Thank you—it does,' said Pop, and we left the under-butler to finish his port.

As we made our way from the kitchen area to the court-room level of the palace I asked Pop what we had learned from Factotum.

'We learned, Sam,' he replied, 'that the good butler was lying to us.'

'How can you be sure of that?'

'We know—from what the late Mr Cairo told us—that at least one person had recently been placed on the palace staff through Cairo's influence—an influence achieved by bribery.'

'Which the butler did not admit.'

'Which the butler could not really admit, since it involved improper conduct on his part. But the *way* a man tells a lie can be revealing to those who have the wisdom to interpret.'

'So you did learn something from him?'

'Solomon says: "Wisdom does more for a man than ten rulers can do for a city".' And that cryptic comment was all I could get out of Pop on the subject.

The room in Herod's palace used as a courtroom was the size of a small banqueting hall.

The high granite walls were draped in flags and regimental standards bearing the Roman eagle. At one end was a high marble bench behind which Governor Felix would sit, facing that were tables for the accused and their legal counsel, and behind those, rows of benches for the public. The whole room was brilliantly lit by oblongs of butter-yellow sunshine that flooded in through high windows on the eastern side.

Paul was already seated at one of the legal tables when we arrived. He was in chains, as he always was when out of his 'prison' suite of rooms, and an armed guard stood behind him. I wasn't sure if this was to prevent Paul from escaping or to protect him from his secret assassin.

The murmur of voices faded as a double-door at the far end of the court opened, and a herald entered.

'Hear ye! Hear ye! All ye who have disputes in need of judgement draw nigh and give attention. This court is now in session, His Excellency Marcus Antonius Felix, Procurator of Judea, presiding.'

At the end of this proclamation a parade of sergeants-at-arms and clerks-of-the-court entered through the double doors. At the end of the procession came Felix: his official robes looking imposing, his manner regal, but his face as shifty and cat-like as ever.

After some ceremonial bowing and scraping the business of the court got underway.

The first case to be heard involved a local merchant. An action had been brought against him by a number of his customers claiming that he was using unfair weights and measures, and that, since he held a monopoly on certain imported goods, they could not deal with him by simply shifting their custom elsewhere.

Felix listened with apparent impartiality as one poorly dressed artisan or farmer after another complained of being cheated by the merchant. Then the richly robed merchant stood up and loudly and vigorously proclaimed his innocence.

At this end of this florid speech Felix instructed the merchant to approach the bench. There the judge and the merchant put their heads together in whispered conversation, at the end of which Felix banged his gavel and announced: 'Not guilty. Next case.'

There was an angry murmur of protest from the public gallery, but this subsided when a sergeant-at-arms thumped his spear on the floor and called for silence. It was clear that Felix had settled this case by accepting an offer of bribery from the wealthy merchant, but nothing could be achieved by protesting about it.

While these preliminary cases were being heard Pop and our client had their heads together, poring over legal documents in whispered consultation.

The next case involved two farmers—one rich and one poor. The wealthy one was claiming ownership of a certain field which the poor farmer was protesting had been in his family for generations. The rich landowner had a document (undoubtedly drawn up by some shifty lawyer) that he claimed was a certificate of title. His poor neighbour had no such documentary proof of his claim, the land in question having simply been handed down from father to son from generation to generation.

This time there was no whispered consultation at the judge's bench (which we all took to mean that the bribe had been paid before the hearing began) and Felix simply ruled in favour of the wealthy landowner with barely a moment's consideration.

Several other civil actions followed—all with similar results.

The civil cases being thus swiftly disposed of, the criminal matters due to be heard were called on. The first was a charge of sedition, and the second involved Paul.

The prisoner accused of sedition was led up before the judge's bench. He was even more heavily chained and manacled than Paul, and, indeed, he looked like

139

a fearsome and dangerous fellow.

A captain of the guard gave the main evidence against the prisoner, namely, that he was an associate and supporter of the notorious revolutionary Eleazar the zealot, and that, as such, he was a member of the *sicarii* —the assassins who struck at their victims in crowded public places with concealed daggers.

When asked to give his defence, the prisoner shouted: 'Death to Romans! Free Judea!' and shook his chains menacingly.

Felix's evil face lit up, and he clearly took great delight in pronouncing a verdict of guilty and a sentence of death. The governor then spent some time consulting his aides on just how this particular death sentence should be carried out.

In the end he ordered that the prisoner be starved for seven days, and then given fifty lashes to make his back bleed, and finally that he be tied to the rocks on the ocean side of the breakwater as shark food.

There was a stunned silence in the court-room as this decision was announced. The sheer cruelty of this governor was breathtaking.

Then, Paul's case was called.

Chapter 20

Tertullus had returned to his lucrative law practice in Jerusalem, leaving the conduct of these recurring court appearances to Demetrius, an oily customer who ran a Caesarean law firm.

Demetrius presented his opening arguments in his usual smoothly sycophantic manner, pushing very hard the point that his clients the Jewish Temple authorities, wanted Paul returned to Jerusalem to face court there. If this application were granted Pop and I knew what would happen: the Forty would revive their original plan, and attempt to ambush and kill Paul on the road.

There was, however, no risk that Felix would agree to this request. For a start it was too legally outrageous for even the slimy governor to agree to, and secondly, with Paul in Jerusalem Felix would lose his opportunity to fish for a substantial bribe.

When Demetrius had finished his opening remarks Paul was invited to address the court. Paul rose to his feet, a figure of great dignity despite the chains that bound him, and in a strenuous effort to appeal to whatever faint glimmer of justice might still flicker inside Felix's heart, made an impassioned speech.

'Your Honour,' said Paul, 'as the Jews are well aware, I was given a thorough Jewish training from my earliest childhood in Tarsus and later at Jerusalem, and I lived accordingly. If they would admit it, they know that I have always been the strictest of Pharisees when it comes to obedience to Jewish laws and customs. But the real reason behind their accusations is something else—it is because I am looking forward to the fulfilment of God's promise made to our ancestors. The twelve tribes of Israel strive night and day to attain this same hope I have! Yet, Your Honour, for me it is a crime, they say! But is it a crime to believe in the resurrection of the dead? Does it seem incredible to you that God can bring men back to life again?

'I used to believe that I ought to do many horrible things to the followers of Jesus of Nazareth. I imprisoned many of the saints in Jerusalem, as authorised by the High Priests; and when they were condemned to death, I cast my vote against them. I used torture to try to make Christians everywhere curse Christ. I was so violently opposed to them that I even hounded them in distant cities in foreign lands.

'I was on such a mission to Damascus, armed with the authority and commission of the chief priests, when one day about noon, sir, a light from heaven brighter than the sun shone down on me and my companions. We all fell down, and I heard a voice speaking to me in Hebrew, "Saul, Saul, why are you persecuting me? You are only hurting yourself".

'"Who are you, sir?" I asked.

'And the Lord replied, "I am Jesus, the one you are persecuting. Now stand up! For I have appeared to you to appoint you as my servant and my witness. You are to tell the world about this experience and about the many other occasions when I shall appear to you. And I will protect you from both your own people and the Gentiles. Yes, I am going to send you to the Gentiles to open their eyes to their true condition so that they may repent and live in the light of God instead of in Satan's darkness, so that they may receive forgiveness for their sins and God's inheritance along with all people everywhere whose sins are cleansed away, who are set apart by faith in me."

'And so, Your Honour, I was not disobedient to that vision from heaven! I preached first to those in Damascus, and then in Jerusalem and through Judaea, and also to the Gentiles that all must forsake their sins and turn to God—and prove their repentance by doing good deeds. The Jews arrested me in the Temple for preaching this, and tried to kill me, but God protected me so that I am still alive today to tell these facts to everyone, both great and small. I teach nothing except what the prophets and Moses said—that the Messiah would suffer, and be the First to rise from the dead, to bring light to Jews and Gentiles alike.'

Suddenly Felix banged his gavel on the bench and shouted, 'Paul, you are insane! Your long studying has broken your mind!'

'I am not insane, Your Honour,' Paul replied quietly. 'I speak words of sober truth.'

But Felix was not listening. 'The prisoner is remanded in custody,' he said. 'This case is adjourned for one week.'

Immediately the governor stood up, and with a swirl of his robes turned towards the double doors that led into his private suite.

'All rise!' bellowed the herald, and as we struggled

to our feet he went on, 'This court now stands adjourned. All persons having further business before the court are hereby commanded to be in attendance on the next day of sitting. Hail the Emperor!'

The soldiers present turned towards the Roman eagle and repeated the herald's salutation: 'Hail the Emperor!' Most of the civilians in the room didn't bother, since the governor was already out of the courtroom there was no need to imitate the foolish Roman ritual.

Our small party made its way under armed escort back to the rooms that constituted Paul's prison. There our client's chains were removed, Silas put on a pot of coffee, and we talked about how the latest round in the trial had gone.

'Your speech was magnificent,' I heard Pop telling Paul. 'You must keep your notes for that; you may be able to use that speech again at some time in the future.'

I wandered away from the main group, and sat down on a broad window ledge to chat to Tim.

I brought Tim up to date on the progress of the case, and then our talk turned to the afternoon's courtroom session.

'I've seen it all before,' I said. 'In fact, I see it every time I am in court with that weasel Felix presiding, but I still feel an ungovernable sense of outrage at the injustice.'

'Yes, I feel exactly the same way,' said Tim. 'When I see behaviour that is so unjust—taking bribes, favouring the rich against the poor, ignoring the merits of the case, ignoring the principles of fairness—something in my heart rebels and says, "It shouldn't be like this!"'

'Exactly! And on top of the injustice is the cruelty.

That revolutionary who was in court today was, I take it, genuinely guilty of sedition. But for Felix to sit there and calmly invent such a cruel death penalty for him was just unbearable.'

'True. He is supposed to be a fair and impartial judge but Felix acts more like a panther—a slinking, predatory cat, stalking a victim.'

'It's interesting that we feel so strongly about unfairness and injustice, isn't it?' I remarked. 'I bet you have a theory about that too, don't you Tim?'

'Now you're making fun of me,' he grinned. 'But as it happens I do believe I know why we are so outraged by injustice.'

'Because God is—I take it—committed to justice?'

'Let me quote something that one of our people in the church at Jerusalem is fond of saying. He says: "Man is destined to die once, and after that to face judgement". Think back to what we were saying about humanity's rebellion against God. This judgement of which I speak is God's response to our rebellion. For God is not like Felix.'

'I take your point. There are some things that *demand* judgement. Because they upset the whole network of just relationships?'

'Exactly. God won't let human beings rebel for ever. God's punishment for rebellion is death and judgement: "Man is destined to die once, and after that to face judgement".'

Chapter 21

Pop and I walked back home from the palace in silence. He was pre-occupied (I think) with Paul's legal problems, and with the mystery of the identity of the Falcon. I was pre-occupied with my conversation with Tim, which I had found disturbing.

That night after dinner I decided that action was the best way to shake off my feeling of depression. So I left the house, determined to do a little sleuthing on my own account—not as just a 'tag-along' assistant to Pop.

It was night-time, and the underworld was at work in back alleys, sleazy bars and deserted warehouses. And that meant it was time for a gumshoe to go to work. It was time for me to start snooping, to follow a few leads, to ask a few questions, to shadow the odd suspect, to stake out the odd joint.

I wanted to prove to Pop that I had the makings of a real detective, and I wanted to polish my skills in preparation for going to work for the Continental Detective Agency.

The neon lights flickered on the wet pavements,

the smell of cabbage floated out of the Lebanese restaurants, nervous cats darted out of the way of stray taxis, and in the distance a dog howled.

Laughing, shouting voices burst out of dimly lit bars like rats escaping from a cage. The air was full of stale beer, cheap wine, and the acrid smell of cigarette smoke.

My first port of call was to find Dash—the best private eye in Caesarea—to pick up a lead.

As usual, Dash was drinking at the *Ad Nauseam*, and I arrived just as a fight was ending. The sawdust on the floor was splattered with blood, and Dash was seated in a corner, his back to the grisly action.

'Why you like drinking in this place I can't imagine,' I said, as I approached his table. Seated opposite Dash was Camillus.

'Oh, it's you, Sam,' said the aristocratic young Roman.

'Take a pew,' said Dash.

I sat down and Dash ordered another round of drinks. I just nursed my glass of hundred-proof poison, knowing I had to keep a clear brain for the night's work ahead of me.

'I like to drink in quiet, soothing surroundings where I feel at home,' said Dash, answering my opening question. He squinted at me through half open eyelids as he spoke. I was never quite sure when he was being serious, and when he was taking the mickey out of me.

'I was born in a very small, quiet town,' Dash went on, 'a sleepy little place called Laudanum. In my first seventeen years I had enough quietness to last a lifetime. Since the day I left home to join the army I haven't been able to relax unless I'm surrounded by noise.'

147

'I see,' I said. 'Now, can I ask you a serious question?'

'Fire away.'

'Is there a particular bar where most of the crims and low-life of Caesarea hang out?'

'There are several,' said Dash. 'Are there any particular crims you're interested in?'

'Those that work for the Fat Man are the ones I'd like to keep an eye on. Where am I likely to find them?'

'Most of them hang around a bar called the *Delirium Tremens*. It's in an alley off Wharf Street. The place is owned by the Fat Man and run for him by a crook named Felonius Caucus.'

'Why do you want this information?' asked Camillus.

'For the Falcon investigation,' I explained. 'While Pop is safely tucked up in bed, I plan on doing a little sleuthing of my own.'

'Initiative!' cried Camillus with delight. 'I like to see that.'

'You've got the makings of a real gumshoe, Sam,' said Dash. 'But you take care. The *Delirium Tremens* makes this place look like a kindergarten. I want you to come back from there with all your major arteries still intact.'

'Don't worry. I can look after myself.'

'Just make sure you do, that's all. I don't want Ben coming to me after he's identified your body, asking why I sent you to that low dive.'

'I'll be careful.'

I left Dash and Camillus doing some serious drinking, and headed towards Wharf Street.

The entrance to the *Delirium Tremens* was no more than a dim glow at the far end of an alley that was as dark as spilt ink at midnight.

When I walked in faces turned to look at me, small candles of suspicion flickering in their eyes. I tried to look casual as I sauntered to the bar and ordered a drink. There was an empty table in the corner, and that's where I took my glass of rot-gut brandy to sit and watch and wait.

After a while the regulars ignored me and went back to their drinking and poker playing. They huddled, heads together, over the small tables, talking in low murmurs.

If these were the citizens of the night, quite frankly, the night was welcome to them: a more scruffy looking bunch I've never seen. And they drank like people who were trying to make sure that the level of blood in their alcohol never got too high.

I sat for a couple of hours, nursing the brandy the health department should have investigated, watching the action, and keeping a look-out for familiar faces.

Late in the evening a weedy young man with a furtive face came through the front door. I recognised him at once as the gunsel known as WC—the Fat Man's chief 'enforcer'.

The gunsel walked with a swagger, as if to advertise his toughness, as he made his way to a front table occupied by a group of poker players. They showed the young hoodlum a surprising amount of respect, or possibly fear, making a place for him at the table and dealing him a hand as soon as he sat down.

After watching for a while it struck me that WC was giving the cards only a fraction of his attention. His gaze kept flickering to the doorway, as though he was expecting someone.

The evening dragged on, the smoke in the air became heavier, and the conversation noisier and drunker.

Close to midnight a couple walked into the bar, and immediately the gunsel stopped playing cards and concentrated his attention on them. This, then, was the arrival he was waiting for.

As the couple stepped forward into the light I recognised the young woman at once. It was Rhea, the Fat Man's daughter! She was stunningly beautiful, in a smouldering and dangerous way. Every eye in the place was on her as she shimmered up to the bar with her companion and ordered two drinks. Rhea knew that she was the centre of attention—and she loved it.

Eventually I dragged my eyes away from the hypnotic beauty to make a study of her companion. The result was a shock of recognition. I knew that young man from somewhere! But from where?

He was slightly taller than average height, with reddish brown hair, and a solid build. Then he leaned across the bar to collect his change and the light hit a distinctive V-shaped scar on his left cheek. It was Caleb! The leader of the Forty!

What was he doing in Caesarea?

There could be only one answer to that question: he was here to pay off the Falcon!

If that was the case, why was he accompanied by Rhea? And why was WC so interested? Just wait, I told myself, just wait and see what happens.

For an hour or so the couple at the bar talked and drank. Rhea giggled a lot and draped herself around Caleb like a clinging vine. She was giving the performance of a woman besotted by her date. It may have been fooling Caleb, but from my sober point of view it was just that—a performance.

At length they left the bar in a clinging, giggling huddle. As soon as they were out the front door the young gunsel got up and followed. I rose from my table determined to follow him in turn. But that's when my luck ran out.

150

At the table right in front of me a fight broke out. Drunken accusations of cheating quickly became fists and elbows whacking into jaws and kidneys. And I found it impossible to wade quickly through the melée of limbs to the front door.

Within moments the whole bar seemed to erupt into a wild free-for-all, with feet and fists flying all over the place. I tried to protect myself from serious injury, and push through to the doorway at the same time.

At one stage, someone grabbed a heavy metal cauldron from behind the bar and flung it across the room. It missed my head by inches. Someone was taking pot shots at me!

By the time I made it through the front door the alley was empty. I sprinted down its short length and into Wharf Street. It was now midnight, and Wharf Street too appeared to be deserted. The only exception was a shadow disappearing fast around a distant corner. This might or might not be my quarry, but it was my only clue so I had to chase it.

I sprinted the length of the street as hard as I could, running lightly on my toes so as to make as little noise as possible. When I turned the corner into a broad thoroughfare lit by dim yellow street lights, the gunsel was at the next intersection. His body language told me that he too was shadowing someone. So the gunsel had his eye on Rhea and Caleb, and I had my eye on the gunsel.

We must have travelled like that for several blocks when I became aware of two facts: that Rhea and Caleb were heading towards the waterfront, and that a heavy fog was rolling in off the sea.

Once I caught a glimpse of the couple under a distant streetlight, but most of the time all I could see was the gunsel, and I just had to hope that he was keeping his eye on the pair in front.

The streets and pavements were wet with sea spray, and in the fog I found it harder and harder to keep track of my quarry. At length I had to admit I had lost track of them.

The gunsel known as WC had disappeared down one of four ways, each of which was wrapped up in a blanket of midnight fog that would hide the darkest secret.

I had lost them! I had to admit that, and turn my weary footsteps for home.

Chapter 22

Under the shower I cursed myself as seven kinds of an idiot. But as I started to calm down, I told myself that the fight in the bar had held me up, and that was sheer misfortune. Besides which, there were one or two interesting things I had learned.

The first was that the payment from the Forty for their hired assassin had arrived in town—carried personally by their leader. And the second was even more sinister: the Fat Man's criminal crew were taking an intimate interest in the proceedings.

As I crawled into bed I tried to deduce the significance of what I had observed, but my brain was too tired, and the minute my head hit the pillow I started punching out the Zs.

The next morning I came down quite late. As I sheepishly approached the kitchen table in search of some remnants of breakfast Pop's voice from over my shoulder startled me.

'Good morning, Sam,' he said, 'or should it be good afternoon?'

'Sorry, but I did oversleep a bit.'

'Don't apologise. You had a long day yesterday—up before dawn and not in bed until well after midnight. Did your night-time investigations yield any results?'

'Some,' I replied, and told him about Caleb and about Rhea and the gunsel.

'Interesting,' said Pop, rubbing his chin thoughtfully.

'What do you think it means, Pop?'

'No doubt we shall all know what it means before very long. And please don't call me Pop!'

'Sorry. What's on the agenda for today?'

'That too is very interesting. Our agenda has been changed at the last minute.'

'How come?'

'Not five minutes ago a courier arrived from the palace inviting us to a morning reception. To meet His Excellency the Governor no less.'

'Really? Am I invited too?'

'The invitation is addressed to us both.'

'Hey, this should be interesting stuff.'

'Indeed it should', said Pop (I mean Ben, I mean my father. . . aw, what the heck—I'll stick with Pop).

'But why?' I asked. 'Have we suddenly made it onto the social register?'

'Nothing so illustrious I fear. The invitation was, in all probability, prompted by yesterday's court appearance. A note attached to the invitation explains that our client, Paul of Tarsus, has also been invited.'

'So, what does it mean?'

'It means that Felix is finding us somewhat slow at offering him a bribe. This little social gathering is, I suspect, intended to oil the operation of our purses so the gold will flow out more readily.'

'And into Felix's numbered Swiss bank account?'

'Precisely.'

'So, do we go anyway?'

'Most certainly we go. We will offer Felix no money, but it is an opportunity to informally argue our case. And, perhaps also an opportunity to observe a little more of how the palace functions, which in turn may help in our hunt for the Falcon.'

'So what sort of reception is this, and when does it start?'

'It's called a "Wine and Cheese Morning", and it begins in a little over an hour from now. So hurry up and finish your coffee and we'll be off.'

On the way to the palace we stopped at our office, so that Pop could check his mail and phone messages and give Zimri his instructions for the day.

On arriving at Herod's palace, we went up to Paul's guarded rooms (where I carefully avoided falling into another conversation with Tim) and made our way down to the reception room with Paul and his party. Paul, of course, had to wear his chains to the reception—they were compulsory whenever he was out of the guarded room.

I thought about this as we walked through the palace. Wouldn't Felix be embarrassed to have one of his guests at a reception wearing the chains of a prisoner? Then I realised that the Governor was used to it: if he fished for bribes as blatantly with all his prisoners as he did with us, he probably entertained chained prisoners at official functions quite often!

The reception was held in a large room lined with dignified marble columns and lit by tall windows that looked out on a sparkling blue sea. It was already half filled with mingling guests and a buzz of conversation. Servants passed among the crowd carrying trays of black olives and small pastries filled with goats' milk cheese (the handiwork of Shallum perhaps?).

I felt a tap at my elbow and turned around to see young Naissa there. She was carrying a tray of tall glasses filled with chilled white wine.

'Good morning Mr Bartholomew,' she said.

'My father is "Mr Bartholomew", Naissa,' I replied. 'Call me Sam.'

'Good morning, Sam,' she returned, with a smile and a giggle.

I was searching for a subject I could chat about when we were interrupted by a blast of trumpets from the far end of the room.

All conversation stopped and we all turned towards the sound. Huge multi-leafed doors at the end of the room swung open as a herald with lungs of brass bellowed: 'Their Excellencies Governor Marcus Antonius Felix and the Lady Drusilla Felix'.

The couple who entered were elegantly, and no doubt expensively, robed. They both jangled as they walked: he with a row of (self-awarded) service medals; she with dangling jewellery worth the annual gross domestic product of one of the smaller nations.

Felix had the haughty look of a low-born freedman who has risen to noble rank, while his wife had the stunning beauty of a Jewish princess illuminated by the freshness of youth—for she was still only nineteen years of age. Soon a crowd of courtiers surrounded them and the general babble of conversation resumed.

I turned to continue my chat with Naissa, but she had gone. Disappointed, I returned to Pop and the rest of Paul's party and joined their circle of conversation.

Some half an hour later an equerry in military dress uniform approached our group and said that the governor would like to speak with us. He then led the way through the crowd to the place where Felix and Drusilla were standing in the midst of an admiring (or at least sycophantic) circle.

'The Jewish prisoner, Your Excellencies,' announced the equerry with a bow.

'Ah, my good sirs,' said Felix effusively, 'I trust that you are enjoying our small social gathering. Just a few intimate friends as you can see,' he added, as with a wide sweep of his arm he gestured towards the crowd that filled the hall.

'We are delighted to be here,' said Pop, replying on behalf of the group, 'And we thank Your Excellencies for the invitation. It is delightful to have an opportunity to discuss the merits of our case in less formal circumstances than a court-room permits.'

'How very true, how very true indeed,' said Felix, with an oily smile. 'And I must tell you, Paul, that you make very impressive speeches in court.'

Paul acknowledged the compliment with a nod of his head.

'As I understand the matter,' continued the governor, 'you are a leader of considerable importance in this new religion thing—whatever it is. That being the case I am sure you must have some wealthy supporters whose resources you could call upon.'

'I am certain that Your Excellency would agree,' interrupted Pop quickly, 'that there are some cases that should be determined upon their merit alone.'

'Quite—quite,' replied Felix sourly.

It was clear that Pop's quick response had headed off any angling for a bribe for the time being.

'Of course it can take some time to decide a case on merit alone,' said Felix with a sly grin. 'But enough of that for the time being. Paul, tell me something of this religion of yours.'

This was an invitation to which Paul was only too ready to respond. Paul, of course, knew, as we all did, something about the rumoured lifestyle of Felix and Drusilla, so he took the opportunity to reason with them about righteousness, and self-control and the judgement to come.

Felix said nothing, but it appeared to me that as Paul went on he became more and more uncomfortable.

After some time, the governor responded to Paul somewhat sharply. 'Go away for now, and when I have a more convenient time I'll call for you again.'

Paul, and the rest of our group, retired just a short distance away from the official party, and another guest was presented to Felix and Drusilla.

As we were standing there Naissa approached with a single golden goblet on a tray. This she offered to Paul, 'Would you like a drink, sir?'

Paul accepted the offer graciously and took the goblet from the tray, but before he could take a drink a uniformed equerry came rushing up and snatched it from his hand.

'Who gave you this?' he demanded, 'This golden goblet is for the exclusive use of His Excellency.' And without waiting for a reply the man stalked off bearing the goblet with him.

I was vaguely aware, just out of the corner of my eye, of the goblet being offered to Theopoulos to taste, and then being handed to Felix.

Suddenly, pandemonium broke out! With a loud cry Theopoulos grabbed at his throat and fell to the ground. An attendant snatched the goblet away from Felix before he could take a sip with a shouted cry of 'The drink is poisoned! Someone is trying to murder His Excellency!'

Chapter 23

The next few minutes were utter chaos. Every courtier, every attendant, every soldier seemed to be shouting and pushing all at once—all trying to prove that they were in the frontline when it came to defending their Governor.

In the shambles that resulted everyone seemed to be ignoring poor Theopoulos who was lying on the floor, writhing in what looked like a death agony. All, that is, except Paul's companion—Doctor Lucas. He knelt by the dying man's side and made a rapid examination.

'I might be able to save him,' said Lucas, 'Tim—fetch my bag!'

Tim took off at a run to fetch the bag from Paul's rooms.

The Lady Drusilla screamed repeatedly, and then broke down into heavy sobbing, while Felix clutched at his chest moaning, 'Oh, oh, oh. The shock has been too much for me. Fetch my physician!'

Doctor Lucas turned to me and said, 'Give me some

help here.' I knelt down beside him and helped to roll Theopoulos over so that his head was facing downwards, then Lucas thrust a finger into the back of the dying man's throat and induced vomiting.

I helped to support Theopoulos's shoulders while he retched, with violent shudders and trembles passing through his body.

Abruptly there was a shriek behind us of 'Not on the tiles! Don't let him vomit on the tiles!', It was Felix, apparently recovered from his shock and in a foul mood.

Pop intervened. 'Your Excellency,' he said, 'this servant has just saved your life. He must be cared for immediately—right here and now—otherwise he will die.'

Reluctantly the governor responded, 'Yes, I suppose you're right. The poor wretch has served me well. You may care for him here, and then bury him in the palace cemetery afterwards. Factotum! See that this floor is cleaned thoroughly when these people have finished.'

Tim ran back into the room carrying Lucas's bag.

'Look for the bottle labelled *Syrup of Ipecac*,' said the doctor, 'and pour a small dose into a cup.'

Tim did this, then I supported Theopoulos while Lucas administered the medicine. The result was immediate and spectacular: more violent vomiting.

'I want a cup of milk into which the whites of two raw eggs have been mixed,' said Doctor Lucas. This order was transmitted to one of the domestic servants who hurried away to the kitchens to prepare the concoction.

The governor's party had moved some distance away from where we were working on the dying man, but we could still hear the shocked tones of their conversations. Suddenly one voice rose above the rest. It was Drusilla: 'Who is the murderer?' she demanded. 'Who tried to kill my husband?'

This provoked a wave of murmured enquiries.

'Where did that goblet come from?'

'From the cellars, I suppose.'

'But who served it? Did anyone have a chance to touch the cup before it was served to His Excellency?'

'It was him!' yelled an attendant loudly at this point. 'He had the cup that was poisoned!'

I looked up and was horrified to see that the man was pointing at Paul!

Every eye in the room was suddenly fixed on our client.

'It's true! It's true!' insisted the attendant. 'I saw that prisoner with His Excellency's golden goblet in his hand and I seized it from him and handed it to the taster.'

'Is this so?' hissed Felix venomously. 'You snake! You viper! Kill him!'

In a flash a soldier had rushed across the room and held a sword poised at Paul's throat.

Paul neither turned nor flinched. He stood his ground courageously, in a dignified silence.

'Your Excellency wait! Wait!' said Pop, rushing up to Felix's side. 'My client held the goblet only for a moment, and only because it was handed to him.'

'Well?' said Felix.

'The poison was meant for him, Your Excellency— not for you!'

'Why would anyone want to poison a prisoner? That makes no sense!'

'That violent group in Jerusalem have been trying to kill my client,' continued Pop, 'as Your Excellency well knows. It is for that reason that Commander Lysias sent him here for trial, rather than keep him in

Jerusalem. And I have been informed that this group has hired a professional assassin to complete the task in which they failed. This attempted poisoning is the result.'

Felix began to look mollified, and he turned to Drusilla and said, 'There you are, my love. We should have realised that no one would try to kill me. My people love me too much.'

We all breathed a sigh of relief as the soldier lowered his sword from Paul's throat.

'You,' said Felix, pointing at Pop, 'will find this assassin so that my soldiers can execute him! Factotum—you will give him whatever assistance he needs. We will not allow such things in our palace. Now, come Drusilla dear, we shall retire to our private chambers.'

As the governor and his wife left the reception hall loud conversations erupted among the spectators.

I returned to Theopoulos's side. Doctor Lucas was attempting external cardiac massage and artificial respiration. 'There is little hope,' said the doctor as he checked his patient's pulse, 'but I shall keep on trying.'

A servant returned with the concoction prescribed by Lucas, but very little of it could be forced down Theopoulos's throat. The taster was deathly pale and very still. I had little doubt that he was dying.

I left Tim and the doctor kneeling beside the patient, and drifted back to Pop's side.

'What now?' I asked.

'We must investigate at once, before these witnesses scatter,' he said. 'Did you, Sam, happen to see who handed Paul that poisoned goblet?'

I looked at Pop but I was unable to answer.

'You did, didn't you?' he said. 'Who was it?'

'Yes, I saw who served that drink. But it couldn't be

her,' I protested. 'She couldn't have had anything to do with it.'

'It was Naissa then,' said Pop.

'We shall beat the truth out of her,' said Factotum as he joined us, his voice heavy and pompous.

'That will not be necessary, I'm sure,' said Pop.

We found Naissa huddled against one of the tall windows, pale and shivering with shock.

'Naissa,' said Pop gently, 'who gave you that golden goblet, and asked you to serve it to Paul?'

A shudder passed through her slender frame, but she continued to look down at the floor and did not speak.

'Speak!' thundered Factotum, 'Or you shall be whipped.'

'Leave this to me!' snapped Pop. 'Naissa, you are not to blame for what happened. It is not your fault. But someone used you to pass on the poisoned drink. You must tell us who that person is, child.'

Slowly Naissa raised her eyes. She did not look at Pop or at Factotum, but at me. 'I can't remember,' she whimpered. 'I've been trying. But I can't.'

'You must try harder,' I urged. 'This is vitally important, Naissa. No one but you can help us with this. Try to remember.'

'I c-c-can't.'

'Think. What were you doing just before you served that drink?'

'I d-d-don't know. I think I had a tray of empty glasses that I was taking back to the bar. . . I think. But I'm not sure.'

'A tray of empty glasses. Right, that's a start. Picture it: you took them back to the bar. . . and then what?'

'I don't know. I c-c-can't remember.'

'Where were you given the golden goblet? Was it at

163

the bar? Or were you somewhere else when it was handed to you?'

'I can't think. I've been trying. Honestly I have. But I just c-c-can't,' and she broke down into hopeless sobbing. I put my arms around her to comfort her, and patted her gently on the back.

'It is useless pushing her any further,' said Pop turning to Factotum. 'The shock has had the effect of suppressing all memory of what happened just before the poisoning. Perhaps it will come back to her later.'

'I can improve her memory at once,' said Factotum, 'A good beating will achieve that.'

'No!' said Pop firmly, 'That will achieve nothing. You are to leave the questioning of this young woman to me!'

'If you insist.'

'I do.'

'Is there any other assistance I can render at this time?' asked the under-butler.

'I think not.'

'Then I must go about my duties.'

And with that he glided silently away from us, like an ocean liner sailing into the sunset.

'I think it's safe to move the patient now,' said Doctor Lucas, 'or at least, we can do him no further harm by moving him.'

'Where should we take him?' asked Tim.

'Back to Paul's rooms,' said the doctor, 'where I can keep an eye on him. He will need constant nursing for the next twenty-four hours. His life signs are very low, very faint indeed. But he is at least stable now.'

'Is there much hope that he will live?'

'Very little I fear,' said Lucas, shaking his head, 'very little.'

Two servants arrived with a stretcher from the

palace infirmary. Several of us lifted the dead weight of Theopoulos onto the stretcher, then with Tim taking one end and I the other, the whole party returned to Paul's rooms.

When we arrived, we found that a heavy cloud had settled upon our spirits leaving us silent and subdued.

It was Pop who broke the silence. 'The question now is: who was the poison really meant for? Paul or Felix?'

Chapter 24

'But,' I protested, 'you told Felix the poison was definitely intended for Paul!'

'What else could I say in the circumstances?' said Pop with a shrug of his shoulders. 'But in my own mind the issue is far from closed.'

'You'd better explain,' I said.

'With pleasure. You agree that this poisoning must be the work of the Falcon.'

'It must be,' I agreed.

'By the way,' said Doctor Lucas, 'the poison used appears to have been arsenic. I would have to conduct a Marsh test on the remaining wine to be certain, but my guess is arsenic.'

'That confirms it then,' I said.

'Agreed,' commented Pop, 'but for whom was the arsenic meant? Paul is the target, true. It is for the death of Paul that the Falcon is being paid by friend Caleb and the Forty. But how did the Falcon intend to achieve that goal?'

'What are the options?'

'He could either strike directly, or else indirectly. Remember what Smarticus told us about the Falcon's *modus operandi*? Namely, that he sometimes chooses to strike in a devious, manipulative, and indirect manner.'

'How does that apply in this case?'

'What would happen if the Falcon could arrange for Governor Felix to be murdered in such a way that Paul appeared to be guilty?'

'Why, Paul would be executed on the spot, of course.'

'Which is what almost happened.'

'That's right!' I said. 'So the plan was to poison the goblet, and have Naissa present it to Paul knowing that one of the governor's attendants would immediately seize it out of Paul's hand and pass it on. Then what? Hope that Felix drank before the arsenic started to work on the taster?'

'But surely that was a rather unreliable plan?' said Tim. 'Wasn't there a risk that Paul would drink the poisoned wine before an attendant claimed it as belonging to the Governor?'

'That's the beauty of the Falcon's plan as I understand it,' said Pop. 'It was designed to work in several ways, depending on the circumstances.'

'What ways?'

'These are the levels or layers of the Falcon's scheme: Firstly, if Paul drank the poisoned wine he would quickly die and the murderer's aim was achieved. Secondly, if the cup was seized from Paul before he could drink, in all likelihood he would be executed within a short time of the governor dying. Thirdly, even if it was the taster, and not the governor, who died, there would still be a chance that Paul would be seen as the would-be poisoner and executed

167

on the spot—which is what almost happened.'

'The Falcon is crazy!' I remarked.

'If he's crazy,' said Pop, 'he's crazy like a fox!'

'This is a twisted mind we're dealing with here.'

'True,' said Pop, 'An evil, twisted, and distorted mind. It is almost as though he likes to play with his victim as a cat plays with a captured mouse. There is great ingenuity in the Falcon's thinking, but also great evil.'

As I thought about what Pop said, what really bothered me was the ability of someone with such a twisted mind to put on a mask, and pretend to be a normal member of society.

I took another look at the barely breathing patient, and then wandered over to a window-seat in the sun. A few moments later I was joined by Tim.

'Dramatic morning,' he said.

'Sure was,' I responded. 'Did you know that Pop and I had spoken to the taster, Theopoulos, only yesterday?'

'No. I didn't know that.'

I repeated our interview with Theopoulos for Tim's benefit. 'It's a remarkable story isn't it?' I said as I concluded. 'Can you imagine being prepared to die for another man? Especially for a thoroughly unpleasant, unjust and cruel man like Felix?'

'Of course,' said Tim, 'that's exactly what Jesus did on a Roman cross outside Jerusalem twenty-four years ago. He was a good person who died for bad people. Because of his love for us, God sent his son Jesus into this world. Jesus always lived under God's rule. He did so perfectly. And then by dying he took our punishment and brought us forgiveness. As Peter says: "Christ died for sins once for all, the righteous for the unrighteous, to bring you to God".'

'But how? How could the death of Jesus—however

many years ago—affect me now?'

'Well, in the death of Jesus there are sure to be some elements beyond our understanding. We're only human. But there is a great deal that we can understand.'

'Like?'

'Well, you can think about the death of Jesus as paying a debt, a debt of moral failure, that humans have accumulated and that he has paid on our behalf. He died the death we deserved to die. . .'

Before he could finish the sentence we were interrupted by Commander Cornelius who hurried into the room waving a crime report on a slip of paper. 'Ben. . . Sam. . . ' he said, '. . . this report just came in. You'll want to come with me to the scene of the crime. This is your case more than mine. Come on, let's go.'

'Go where?' I asked. 'What has happened?'

'That chap from Jerusalem you told me about,' said Cornelius, 'that Caleb—he's been found murdered!'

Chapter 25

As we sat in the back of a speeding police car Cornelius explained, 'They found him in a sewer down near the waterfront. His head and all his limbs had been severed.'

Pop and I looked at each other—we both knew what that meant.

We came to a halt in a street called the Heroes of Actium Parade, which ran parallel to the harbour wharfs. In the middle of the street a number of official vehicles were parked around an open manhole.

Cornelius flashed his badge at the junior city watch officer standing guard over the manhole, who responded by giving us the nod to proceed. We stepped over the round, heavy, metal cover that had been removed from the opening and was now lying on the road, and began climbing down the narrow ladder that descended into the bowels of the sewers.

We emerged into a vast concrete tunnel, some fifteen feet in diameter. A hundred yards from the base of the ladder we found the official party grouped around the corpse.

Captain Rufus Metellus was in charge.

'Afternoon, sir,' he said, as he saluted Cornelius, and turning to us he added, 'afternoon, gentlemen. This is a messy one, this is.'

He stood to one side and showed us the body. It was pretty grim: the work of a professional killer who enjoyed practising his trade. The arms had been severed at the shoulders, and the legs just above the knees. The severed head, with an expression of sheer terror frozen on its face, was a few feet away.

I looked up at Pop. His mouth was fixed in a hard, straight line, and I knew he was angered by this senseless slaughter.

My stomach was starting to churn over, and I tried to cope with the horror by making light of it.

'Well,' I said, 'this *corpus* is not very *delecti*!'

Cornelius looked at me sympathetically. He knew I was joking to cover the sickness I felt in the pit of my stomach.

'I've seen this sort of thing before,' said Captain Metellus. 'It's a gangland killing—the work of the Fat Man's "enforcer".'

The police surgeon, Dr Neronius Nausea joined our group. 'Do you want me to tell you the cause of death?' he asked.

'Only if you can surprise us,' replied Cornelius.

'The cause of death was decapitation,' said Dr Nausea.

'You haven't surprised us,' said the commander.

'I've finished here,' added the doctor, 'so the mortuary people can remove the body if you wish.'

Captain Metellus gave orders to this effect.

'How was the body found?' asked Pop.

'Two Sewerage Department workers came across

it this morning in the course of their routine work,' said Metellus.

'And when did he die?' asked Pop, turning to the doctor.

'Hard to say, very hard to say,' said Dr Nausea. 'The massive blood loss would have caused a very rapid drop in body temperature, making the usual scale unreliable. I'll examine the stomach contents later, that may tell me something about the time of death.'

'I saw him drinking in a bar about eleven o'clock last night,' I said, hoping this information might be useful.

'Well, there you are then,' said Dr Nausea. 'Death occurred sometime between eleven o'clock last night and. . . say. . . six o'clock this morning as the latest time.'

'A broad margin,' commented Pop.

'I'll try to narrow it down at the autopsy,' said the doctor, who then made his farewells and left us.

'Ben, would you agree with Captain Metellus here, that this is the handiwork of the Fat Man?' asked Cornelius.

'I'm certain it is,' murmured Pop thoughtfully. 'In fact, I am so certain that I am going to pay a call on that gentleman—immediately.'

'I had formed exactly the same intention,' said Captain Metellus. 'Can I give you a lift?'

All four of us, Cornelius, Metellus, Pop and myself, travelled by police car across town to the Fat Man's villa on snob hill.

In front of the imposing iron gates, Cornelius pressed the button on the intercom.

'Yeah? Who is it? And whadda ya want?' squeaked the speaker set into the wall beside the gate.

'This is Commander Cornelius. Open up in the name of the Emperor!'

The response was a long, deafening silence.

'Shall I blow the lock off the gate, sir?' asked Captain Metellus, taking out his high-powered service revolver.

'Wait Captain, just wait,' cautioned Cornelius with a sly smile. 'We have to give them time to get over their panic, and to stuff their illicit secrets into a locked vault—then they'll open up.'

And he was right.

After several minutes the huge iron gates swung open, and one of the Fat Man's hoodlums stepped out, looking rather flushed and sounding puffed.

'The boss says you're to come in,' he said, looking up and down the street for our reinforcements. He was clearly relieved to discover only the four of us.

We followed his lead inside the gates, then he turned and (perhaps out of habit) made as if to frisk us for weapons.

'Don't try that on!' snapped Cornelius. 'Just take us to the Fat Man.'

The hoodlum knew not to argue, and he turned and led the way.

After a journey through the labyrinth of corridors we were admitted to the palatial office where the huge man behind the huge desk did not bother to rise when we entered.

'Commander, Captain, Ben, Sam—greetings to you all,' he rasped out. 'To what do I owe this unexpected pleasure?'

'Not unexpected,' said Captain Metellus angrily. 'When you order a murder you know to expect a visit from the authorities!'

The bulbous fat on the swollen body quivered silently for a moment, and then he replied, 'We begin well, sir. I approve of plain speaking, sir, approve of it absolutely. Whose death am I supposed to have encompassed on this occasion?'

'Papers on the body identified the victim as Caleb Eliphaz,' said Metellus.

'The name means nothing to me, sir, indeed less than nothing,' replied the Fat Man, the bulbs of his neck and cheeks all moving independently as he spoke.

'And the investigations conducted by Sam and Ben Bartholomew,' continued the Captain, 'tell us that this man was the leader of a band of conspirators known as the Forty.'

'We will get along better, sir, if you understand that I have nothing to do with conspiracies. Grubby politics fail to interest me. I am simply a man of business, gentlemen, that and nothing more.'

'Then will we talk about business? About money?' asked Metellus.

'We will, sir, that we will. Now you are speaking a language in which I am fluent.'

'Mr Bartholomew's investigations suggest that the victim was carrying a large sum of money when he arrived in Caesarea. There was no money found on his body—none at all. As a businessman, as a fat, greasy, greedy businessman did you consider it good business to order his murder and take his money?'

'Come, come, sir. Let us not descend into low invective. And the answer to your questions, sir, is that I deny everything. If I have unexpectedly come into a large sum of money recently, I insist that I won it gambling on the chariot races. And if you wish to know more I suggest that you contact my lawyer.'

'If we can pin this murder on your gunsel, I'll make sure we track it back to you!'

'Idle threats fail to worry me. Are you suggesting

that there was an eyewitness to this murder? Or that fingerprints or other physical evidence was found at the scene? If so, produce your evidence, sir, and make your arrest.'

The Fat Man knew that Captain Metellus was bluffing. The 'enforcer', WC, was a professional killer: there would be no eyewitnesses and no physical evidence.

'Whether we can touch you on this one or not,' said Cornelius, quietly intervening, 'we want you to know that we are aware of your activities. We have considerable resources, great determination, and endless patience: you will not be safe for ever.'

The bulbous pink face took on a worried expression.

'We'll take up no more of your time,' said Cornelius, 'for the time being, that is.' And he and Captain Metellus turned to leave.

Pop lingered behind them for a moment, and when they were out of earshot he turned to the Fat Man and said, quietly, 'You are playing a dangerous game, a very dangerous game indeed. I hope you realise that. However, the damage is done, and there is no undoing it. I hope you are aware of the risk you face, and are prepared for the consequences.'

'By Gad, sir, you're a character, that you are!' said the Fat Man, with a forced and unconvincing laugh. 'Yes, sir, there's never any telling what you'll say next, except that it's bound to be something astonishing.'

As we turned and followed the two soldiers out of the office, the Fat Man was mopping his brow with a large white handkerchief, and all his bulbs were quivering.

Sitting in the back of the police car, as we drove away from the Fat Man's villa, I turned to Pop and asked, 'What did you mean by that remark? What

175

were you warning him about?'

'The claws of the Falcon. That is what my warning concerned,' he replied.

'What do you mean, Ben?' asked Cornelius.

'The Fat Man was incensed to learn that the empire's most notorious hitman was operating on *his* territory, without either his knowledge or his permission. And in response he has intervened in the Falcon's operation.'

'So, the Fat Man believes he should have been offered a pay-off by the Falcon?' I asked.

'Precisely,' said Pop. 'And in lieu of a pay-off he has extracted his own fee: he has stolen the whole payment from the Forty intended for the Falcon, and he has murdered the messenger bearing the payment.'

'So where does the danger come in?'

'The Falcon will have to strike back. He has no choice. His reputation would be hopelessly damaged if the word spread, as it surely would, that his payments could be ripped-off by local hoodlums.'

'And what form will the Falcon's revenge take?'

'That I cannot guess. But I imagine that we will know very soon.'

Chapter 26

An hour later Captain Metellus had returned to his duties with the city watch, and Cornelius, Pop and myself were gathered in Cornelius's office in the palace.

As the Commander's secretary served three cappuccinos, Cornelius said, 'Well, Ben, I'd like you to bring me up to speed on this case. What do we know so far?'

'All the details? Or the overview?'

'It's your case not mine, dear brother, (for which I am very grateful!): so all I need is an overview.'

'Fine. The story so far then, as we understand it, runs like this. Four weeks ago Paul was falsely accused of defiling the Temple in Jerusalem.'

'What exactly did they say he had done?'

'The charge was that he had taken non-Jews into an area of the Temple where non-Jews are forbidden, on pain of death, to go.'

'And the charge was false?'

'Completely. They had seen Paul with a non-Jew

177

from Ephesus, a man named Trophimus, in the streets of the city, and later, when Paul was in the Temple, they simply *assumed* that he had brought Trophimus in with him.'

'An assumption based on existing ill will, I presume?'

'Precisely. I don't know how serious they were with that charge. I suspect it was a malicious fabrication, a mere excuse to seize a man they had long wanted to get their hands on.'

'Their desire then is to silence Paul?'

'Correct. The charge having been made, the rabble were being incited to a lynching when Paul was rescued from their hands by the Roman Commander in Jerusalem, Claudius Lysias. The next day Lysias took Paul before the Jewish Council for a preliminary hearing. Again there was a great uproar and Paul spent that night in protective custody in the barracks.'

Pop paused to sip his coffee, and then continued.

'That's the background. Shall I go on?'

'Yes please, Ben,' said Cornelius. 'Keep going.'

'Well, the next development was the murder plot by the Forty against Paul, the reporting of this plot by Paul's nephew, and the decision by your opposite number in Jerusalem, Commander Lysias, that Paul would be safer here in Caesarea. We thought the murder plot would end there, but we now know that the Forty went to Tertullus, a notoriously shady member of my own profession, I'm sorry to say. Tertullus, through his knowledge of the underworld, was able to make contact with the Falcon and offer him a contract to murder Paul.'

'This was when? Four weeks ago now?'

'Right,' said Pop. 'Once again Paul's nephew heard of the plan and alerted us. Meanwhile, the Falcon had arrived in Caesarea and, through the connivance of the late Mr Cairo, had gained access to the palace for either himself or an accomplice—we still cannot be sure which—'

'Or perhaps both? Is that possible, Pop?' I interrupted. 'Bearing in mind that six people have been hired in the last few weeks could *two* of them be part of the plot?'

'At this stage we cannot rule out that possibility. Our investigations alerted both Mr Cairo and the Fat Man to the presence of the Falcon in the city. Mr Cairo tried blackmail and died. The Fat Man has stolen from the Falcon, and the repercussions of that are still to be felt.'

'How did the Fat Man pull it off?' I asked.

'Through his network of informers, I would suspect. It would not have been hard for him to identify the leader of the Forty through his contacts with the criminal element in Jerusalem, and to arrange for a signal to be sent when Caleb set out for Caesarea.'

'Then Rhea was dispatched to waylay the helpless young man,' I suggested, 'with her seductive beauty, and, once he was in their hands, WC was under instructions to kill him and take the money he was carrying—the Falcon's fee?'

'Something like that,' agreed Pop.

'Will the Falcon continue his plans to assassinate Paul, now that his fee has been intercepted?' asked Cornelius.

'It would be unsafe on our part to assume that he will desist,' replied Pop, 'for two reasons. First, he may have issued instructions and begun a process which cannot now be stopped. Secondly, he may continue with his mission, confident that he will be able to collect his fee—on pain of death—when he has succeeded.'

'So our vigilance over our brother Paul must not cease?'

'It must not.'

'And how close are you to discovering the Falcon's identity?' asked the commander.

'Closer than we were. The Falcon remains shrouded in mystery, drawing, as it were, a cloak of invisibility about himself. Trying to identify him is like groping one's way through a heavy fog. But we are making progress, and we will soon be able to light a candle in the darkness to illuminate his evil face.'

Pop's confidence amazed me. Personally, I was still as baffled as I had been at the beginning of the case. Was he boasting? Or could he see something that I could not see?

We finished our coffee and left Cornelius to get on with the work that was piling up on his desk.

Pop had to return to our office: the regular work of the law practice was still there, and some of it had become pressing. I, on the other hand, wanted to visit Paul's rooms to see how poor Theopoulos was doing.

When the guards admitted me to the rooms where Paul was held, I saw at once that Theopoulos was still lying on the couch near the window—motionless.

'How is he?' I asked Doctor Lucas.

'Alive,' was the reply, 'but barely. His vital signs are as low as they could be without ceasing altogether. He has not regained consciousness. The prospects for his survival are not good.'

'I'm sorry to hear that,' I said, as Tim walked over.

'So he's still no better?' I said, nodding in the direction of the patient.

'If anything, a little worse,' said Tim, 'Lucas has done all he can for the man, but even medical science has its limits. And knowing that the resources of medicine have been exhausted, we are about to pray for this man's healing.'

'You mean—by divine intervention?'

'Don't you think God could heal Theopoulos, if he wanted to?'

'I've never really thought about it.'

'Well, think about it now. If God made every molecule in your body could he not then, if he wished, re-make those molecules when attacked by poison or illness?'

'If God is really God,' I admitted, 'then logically, he could. But you keep saying "if he wished". Does God really want anyone to die?'

'Of course he wants people to die!' said Tim with a cheerful laugh. 'Look. God can take anything—no matter how evil—and bring good out of it.'

'Even death?'

'Even death. God can turn death into an entry into a new life—life in another dimension. Because Jesus conquered death on our behalf, death is no longer a wall, it is a doorway, a doorway that leads to direct, immediate, personal contact with *him*. Often I have heard Paul say that to be absent from the body—which is what physical death is—is to be present with the Lord. Anyway, we're going to pray for Theopoulos now. Would you like to join us?'

'But if death can be such a good thing, what are you actually going to pray for?'

'We are going to ask that God's will be done. Do you want to join us?' asked Tim.

So I stayed as Paul and his group sat around the dying man's bedside and prayed for him. I just sat and listened. I was amazed at the way they prayed. They just sort of, well, chatted to God the way I would chat to a friend.

And their very real concern for poor Theopoulos was moving. Clearly, they had far more compassion for the Official Taster than His Excellency, Governor Felix, ever had!

The other thing that amazed me was how long they prayed. They actually seemed to enjoy it.

At last they stopped, and I took my farewells and headed home.

As I walked through our front door the delicious smell of the evening meal came wafting out of the kitchen.

'Hey that smells great, Mom,' I said as I sauntered into the kitchen at the back of house, 'What's for dinner tonight—You? What are you doing here?'

This remark will strike you as odd if you had been expecting, as I had been expecting, that the person in the kitchen would be my mother. After seeing my mother in the kitchen for the past twenty-two years I have worked out by now what she is doing there.

My remark, therefore, needs further explanation. And here it is: the person I discovered stirring a large pot on our kitchen stove was Naissa. She of the soft, pale skin and flashing dark eyes.

Under these circumstances, 'What are you doing here?' is a reasonable question.

'I work here now', she said, with a smile that would make the angels sing (at least, if I were an angel I would, upon glimpsing that smile, grab three other angels and become an instant barber shop quartet).

'Your father offered me a job,' she continued, in a voice that I now noticed for the first time had a strangely musical quality about it. 'He said I would enjoy working in a smaller establishment better than at the palace. So, he offered me a job, and I said yes, and here I am. Don't you approve?'

'Me? Approve? Absolutely! I couldn't possibly approve more! Do you like it here?'

'Well, I've only been here for half a day so far. But your mother is just so sweet, and your sister Naomi is the same age as me, and she's been really nice too, and we're getting along really well.'

'And then there's me,' I said. 'That's an added bonus attraction that you don't get in every household.'

Naissa laughed, and I could see that this arrangement was going to work out fine.

Just then Pop walked into the kitchen, and I congratulated him on his new hiring policy. He beckoned me out into the lounge room, and when we were alone he said, 'Naissa is here for her own safety.'

'What do you mean?'

'Whoever handed her that poisoned drink this morning is either an agent of the Falcon, or the Falcon himself.'

'Has she remembered who it was yet?'

'Not yet. But she will in time. And the Falcon knows that as well as we do. And he knows that he can continue to be safe only if he kills Naissa.'

'Just as he killed Mr Cairo?'

'Just as, I imagine, he has killed many people over the years. Whoever discovers his identity he kills: that is how he covers his tracks so completely. I have brought Naissa to our house to save her life.'

Chapter 27

That night I had difficulty sleeping, worrying about the fate of Theopoulos.

At about midnight I got out of bed and pulled my clothes back on. My plan was to return to the palace and offer to sit with Theopoulos, while Lucas and the others got some sleep.

Out in the streets the air was warm and still. The chill damp weather of the past few nights having blown away, the soft, balmy Mediterranean air had once again embraced the city.

The full moon hung in the sky like a silver denarius, a perfect circle of phosphorescence low over the sea, walking upon the waves. Looking seaward, there was a shimmering silvery path where the moonlight turned ripples into diamonds.

I strode down the middle of the deserted and desolate streets towards the palace. Most of the houses I passed were plunged into darkness. And the darkness seemed to seep into my very heart and I sank into gloomy forebodings, the source of which I could not explain.

At the palace the huge, multiple-leaf doors that stand open all day were now closed and locked. But a small watchman's door set into one of the leaves was open, and guarded by a uniformed sentry.

It took me several minutes to talk my way in. I had to produce some identification and explain the purpose of my visit at that unearthly hour.

Inside I made my way up the main marble staircase—by day flooded with sunlight and swarming with people, but now echoing with emptiness and lit only by dim night lights and the pale milky glow of moonlight falling through high windows. On the second floor I turned towards the northern, or military, wing of the palace, and soon came to the rooms in which Paul was held.

Fortunately the corporal on duty at the door recognised me, produced his keys, unlocked the heavy padlock that secured the door overnight, and allowed me to enter.

Inside, Paul, Doctor Lucas and Tim were sitting around the motionless form of Theopoulos. Clearly, an all-night vigil was being held at the bedside of the dying man.

They acknowledged my arrival with some surprise, and I joined them.

'How is he?' I asked.

'Fading slowly,' replied the doctor.

I reached out and touched the patient's hand. It was alarmingly cold. Surely this was the chill, I thought, of death.

'Is he. . . ?' I began to ask.

'He is still alive,' said Lucas, interpreting my thoughts, 'but only just. The early hours of the morning are likely to be the crisis time.'

185

'Can I help?' I said, 'Perhaps if I'm here, one or more of you can get some sleep.'

Doctor Lucas accepted my offer.

'Although the patient's extremities are cold,' he explained 'his brow is feverish, and it needs to be wiped with a damp cloth every few minutes.'

He handed me the cloth he had been using and I took his place at Theopoulos's side.

'But the main thing,' continued Lucas, 'is to keep an eye, or an ear, on his breathing and summon me immediately if there is any change.'

I promised that I would, and then, at Paul's insistence Lucas retired to the adjoining room to sleep.

Paul sat at a nearby table, from which he could keep one eye on the patient while reading a scroll of the scriptures by the light of a small lamp. Tim sat on the other side of the couch, across from me, and took turns at bathing the patient.

In this way the long watches of the night slowly passed.

If you had asked me why I had come, I don't think I could have explained. It was just something I had to do. Somehow I had felt uncomfortable about lying in a warm bed, in oblivion, while the poisoned man fought for life.

At length the oblongs of blackness that were the windows in the northern wall of the room faded into a dark gray, and then into a paler gray. Soon a cock could be heard to crow in the distance, and still the crisis had not come—the patient continued his faint, shallow breathing.

In time, a pink glow, like a fire of rose petals, began to burn in the sky, and the horizon became faintly visible. The furthest point that could be seen through those north facing windows was the distant summit of

Mount Carmel. As the sun rose a crucible of liquid gold was emptied over that distant peak. Slowly the golden light flowed down the sides of the mountain and trickled into the valleys. Soon the sky was a pale blue, and the new day had been born.

A sudden groan from the patient startled me.

'Fetch the doctor, quickly,' I said to Tim.

Theopoulos moaned again, and his shoulders began to move restlessly upon the couch. As his eyelids tried to feebly flicker open a sleepy Doctor Lucas knelt down and examined him.

'Fetch a cup of water,' said the medical man, and Tim hurried off.

When he returned the patient's head was lifted and the cup was held to his lips. To my astonishment, as the water trickled into his mouth Theopoulos began to drink.

'Just take small sips,' said Lucas, and then, after a minute he added, 'That's enough for now.'

Then Lucas took one of the patient's hands and began vigorously rubbing the wrist to revive warmth and circulation. On his instruction I did the same to the other hand.

'Bring some more blankets,' Lucas called to Tim. 'We need to wrap him up as warmly as we can.'

'What's happening?' I asked.

'The crisis has passed,' explained the doctor, 'Theopoulos will live.'

Theopoulos will live!

I was amazed and delighted at the same time. Looking more closely at the poisoned taster I could see, and hear, that his breathing was indeed deeper and more regular than it had been on my arrival at midnight.

'An answer to prayer,' I said, trying to talk the

theological jargon of these people.

'Yes,' said Lucas as he tucked some thicker blankets around the patient, 'it's certainly that.'

'So,' I said, 'Theopoulos was healed by God's direct and miraculous intervention?'

Doctor Lucas surprised me by replying, 'I don't know exactly what healed him. It may have been a direct intervention by God. Or it may have been my medical treatment. Or it may have been Theopoulos's own hardy physique. In fact, it was probably a combination of all three. But, whatever the mechanism of his healing, it is God who did it. God gave the world medical knowledge, God gave Theopoulos a hardy physique, and God can (and does) directly intervene at a molecular level to change the course of an illness, whatever the mechanism of healing God is behind it.'

Once the patient had been made comfortable Paul led the group in a prayer of thanksgiving to God for Theopoulos's survival of the crisis, and for his continued recovery.

Then Paul retired to catch up on some sleep. Doctor Lucas went off to the kitchen to order an invalid meal for Theopoulos, and Tim and I continued to sit beside the couch where the poisoned taster had now fallen into a deep, healthy sleep.

'He was as good as dead, Tim,' I said, 'about as near to the grave as anyone could get, and still survive.'

'We Christians believe in someone who not only survived, but triumphed over death. Someone who was stone cold dead, buried in a rock tomb, and who came back to life,' responded Tim. 'This is what lies at the very heart of the story of Jesus. Not only did he die on our behalf—to win our rescue, and ransom, and reconciliation with God—but he also conquered death on our behalf.'.

'Yes, but people do not conquer death. It just doesn't happen. Go down to the city cemetery any day—or night for that matter—you'll find it's a pretty quiet place. Those dead people just lie there in their graves. That's what dead people do. I know that my father investigated the so-called resurrection of Jesus from the dead. In fact, it was his very last case before he gave up being a private eye, married Mom, and settled down to practise law. And I know his report on that case is around the place somewhere, but to be honest I have never read it.' *

'You should. When Peter was talking about this to a group of us in Jerusalem once he said: "In his great mercy God has given us new birth into a living hope through the resurrection of Jesus Christ from the dead". This means that Jesus—who is God—is stronger than death. And our great hope for eternal life is that he defeated death on our behalf.'

*See *The Case of the Vanishing Corpse.*

Chapter 28

Tim and I continued to argue about the death, burial and resurrection of Jesus—what really happened and what it really meant—as we walked across the road to *Herod's Leftovers* for breakfast. We continued the debate all the way through the hot rolls and coffee, and all the way back to the palace again.

At the palace steps I took my leave of Tim and caught a bus across town to the office sign-posted by the brass plate which read: "Ben Bartholomew, Attorney at Law".

It was some days since I had done any work at all in my capacity as an articled clerk to Pop, and I was starting to feel a little guilty about this. The weight of duty was pressing upon my shoulders, and I could ignore it no longer.

I arrived to find Pop already at work at his desk and Zimri busy in the outer office.

The next few hours passed quickly with Pop talking to clients, both on the telephone and in the office, me preparing a number of documents for lodgement at the Registrar General's office at the palace, and Zee looking after the callers, the files and the correspondence.

One of our clients, a big property owner named Nebulus Nimbus, had been negotiating to buy a hotel in a little Roman seaside resort, and now the deal looked like falling through.

We managed to get Nimbus's deal back on the rails, and, in addition, by mid morning we had stitched up the last details of a contract between our client, the well known author Arthur Apocrypha, and the big publishing house of Barabbas and Company.

And by midday we had caught up on the whole of our back-log of work.

'A most productive morning, Sam and Zimri,' said Pop, 'Thank you both. And now, having got that out of the way, I can return to the problem of the Falcon. Sam, are you coming with me to the palace?'

Of course I was going with him to the palace. From Pop's comment to Cornelius the night before I had a feeling in my bones that the case was reaching a climax.

As our cab pulled up in front of the palace steps Camillus, the man I thought of as my future employer, came out of the entrance and stepped into a chauffeur-driven limousine. I waved to him, but he didn't see me.

In Paul's rooms we found Theopoulos awake and sitting up.

'How are you feeling now?' I asked.

'Pretty shaky,' he replied. 'I'm feeling as weak as a kitten, and I have this foul taste in my mouth.'

'You're fortunate to be alive,' I reminded him.

'Oh, I realise that,' he said with a faint smile, 'and I'm very grateful to Doctor Lucas.'

Theopoulos yawned widely, and showed every sign

of wanting to fall asleep again, so I left him and found a seat for myself on a window ledge in the sun.

Paul and Pop were deep in conversation, Titus and Silas were working on Paul's voluminous correspondence, the weary Doctor Lucas was resting in the next room, and Tim was out on an errand of some sort.

Having no one to talk to I sat by myself in the sun, and soon began falling asleep in the gentle warmth. In a half-sleeping, half-waking state I found my thoughts turning to Naissa. By closing my eyes I could see her in my imagination: soft, lustrous dark hair, warm brown eyes, soft skin, stunning smile.

I was startled from my pleasant half-doze by the arrival of lunch: a large, steaming tureen full of minestrone soup, and a plate stacked high with warm, crusty, fresh bread.

We all served ourselves and then Paul gave thanks for the food. As we started to eat Pop remarked, 'You appeared to drop off to sleep in the sun there, Sam.'

'I admit it,' I said. 'But in my own defence I must point out that I had no sleep last night—none at all.'

Before anyone else could join in ribbing me over my sleepiness one of the kitchen servants arrived, the woman Cassandra, with a bottle of red wine and half a dozen goblets on a tray. Minestrone, crusty bread, and red wine was regarded by our Roman rulers as the ideal lunch.

Cassandra stayed long enough to pour the wine and pass around the goblets.

I was standing beside Pop as Paul picked up his goblet and raised it towards his lips.

'Don't!' shouted Pop, 'Don't drink it, Paul!'

Paul lowered the goblet and turned to Pop, looking puzzled.

'Guards! Seize that woman!' snapped Pop, spinning

around and pointing at the retreating Cassandra.

The small, middle-aged Greek woman showed a surprising amount of fight. She kicked, bit and struggled as two of the guards seized her by the arms and dragged her back from the doorway.

'What's going on?' asked Tim, as he walked in upon this dramatic scene.

'This woman is to be placed under arrest,' said Pop, adding, as he picked up Paul's goblet, 'and this wine is to go to the Official Alchemist for analysis.'

'But why?' I asked, my head spinning. 'What's going on?'

'The Falcon has just tried to earn forty-thousand denarii by murdering Paul. Analysis will show this goblet to be loaded with arsenic.'

'You mean this woman here. . . this Cassandra. . . is. . . ?' I stuttered, in stunned disbelief.

'Yes,' said Pop quietly. 'This is the Falcon.'

We all turned and looked at her: shorter than average height, thin, and sour faced. This was the Falcon?

Suddenly everyone was talking at once.

'But I thought she was a "he". . . ?'

'Are you sure?'

'What's the evidence?'

'But I don't understand. . . ?'

'Somebody call the Commander!'

In the midst of this hubbub Cassandra stopped struggling, and the guards released her arms. A moment later she lunged forward—not towards the door, which was well guarded, but towards the table. Taking us all by surprise, she grabbed the goblet intended for Paul, and drank the contents in a single draught.

In a moment she had collapsed to the floor, and the

room fell into a stunned silence that lasted for seconds and felt like hours.

'Fetch Lucas—quickly,' snapped Pop, breaking the silence.

Tim rushed into the next room, woke up the sleeping doctor, and dragged him to where Cassandra lay.

Shaking his head to clear it of sleep, and rubbing his eyes, Lucas knelt down and examined the small, frail body. 'What happened?' he asked.

Several people explained at once. As soon as he had sorted out the different voices, and understood, Lucas returned to his examination.

'That goblet,' he said at last, 'must have contained a massive dose. She is beyond help. Lift her onto the couch and try to make her comfortable, but there is nothing I can do for her.'

Despite his gloomy prognosis Doctor Lucas worked on his murderous patient for half an hour before admitting defeat and pronouncing life extinct.

By then, Commander Cornelius had arrived in Paul's rooms, along with Captain Metellus, Dr Neronius Nausea, and two attendants from the mortuary unit. The room was as crowded as the Forum on market day.

Once Dr Nausea had confirmed Dr Lucas's diagnosis of the cause of death, and taken the body away, the remaining crowd in the room gathered around Pop to hear his explanation.

'Are you certain that Cassandra is, or was, the Falcon?' asked Cornelius.

'Quite certain,' said Pop.

'But there's more to it than that, isn't there?' I said.

'Yes, Sam, there is,' admitted Pop. 'It is most perceptive of you to recognise that.'

'Spill the beans then Ben,' insisted Cornelius.

'What's the rest of the story?'

'Cassandra is—or was—the Falcon. But she was only half of the Falcon.'

'You've lost me,' complained Cornelius.

'There are two of them!' I crowed in triumph. 'That's it, isn't it Pop?'

'Well done, Sam,' he replied. 'That's it exactly. After considering the evidence supplied by Smarticus, and drawn from sources all over the empire, I concluded that the complete invisibility of the Falcon could best be explained if the Falcon were not one person but two.'

'With one person carrying out part of the operation, and the other person another part!' I interjected.

'Precisely,' said Pop. 'And if the two appeared to have no connection with each other, if they only ever met and conferred in secret, then their separate activities could never be added together and found to equal the Falcon.'

'So, this Cassandra woman is one of those people?' asked Cornelius.

'Yes. She is half of the Falcon. I surmise that the Falcon's murders were divided into two parts: planning and execution. One person was the Falcon's "head" and the other the Falcon's "hand".'

'And Cassandra was the hand of the Falcon?'

'She was. Who better to infiltrate and administer poison that a nondescript, middle-aged Greek servant woman who went unnoticed by everyone except when she complained?'

'So Cassandra's role was to blend into the kitchen staff, and carry out the orders she was given?'

'That's right,' said Pop. 'Remember Sam, in her conversation with us she boasted of having once worked for a noble Roman family. Well, many of the noble families employ a "staff poisoner" so to speak—someone whose task is, under orders, to kill important rivals of the family in the bitter feuds that divide Roman nobility. And often the "staff poisoner" is a Greek, and a woman, since they come from a culture in which the arts of poisoning are learned along side the arts of drugs, and herbs, and healing.'

Doctor Lucas nodded in agreement when Pop said this.

'But how did you know that Cassandra was the one we were looking for?' I asked. 'How did you know that she—and not one of the other servants we interviewed—was the "hand" of the Falcon who had infiltrated the palace?'

'Because of the clue that Factotum gave us,' said Pop. 'When he listed the recent staff appointments, do you remember what he said?'

'It'll be here in my notebook somewhere,' I said, pulling the book out of my pocket. 'Yes. Here it is. You asked him who he had employed recently, and he replied: "There's a Roman, a Greek, a Jew, two Egyptian women and a local girl".'

'Now, think about what he said, and about the people we met. The Roman was Petronius, the Greek was Theopoulos, the Jew was Shallum, and the local girl was Naissa. Who then were the two Egyptian women? He can only have meant Vashti and Cassandra. Now Vashti really is Egyptian, but what made him imagine that Cassandra—with her very Greek name—was Egyptian? Surely because she had been brought to the palace *by an Egyptian*.'

'Mr Cairo!'

'Exactly. Mr Cairo must have slipped a bribe to Factotum, and asked him to find a job in the kitchens for a "relative" of his—Cassandra.'

196

'Who was then assumed by Factotum to be Egyptian like Mr Cairo!'

'Indeed. Furthermore, can you remember what Cassandra told us her job was?'

'Hang on. That'll be here in the notebook too,' I flipped over a few pages and found the note, 'She said: "I'm a cup-bearer under the direction of the cellar master".'

'And who would have handed Naissa that poisoned chalice at the governor's reception to pass on to Paul?'

'Of course! Naissa would have been most likely to accept such a task from an official cup-bearer!'

'Such as Cassandra. Those two clues told me that Cassandra was half the Falcon—the half that infiltrates and executes the murders planned by the other half. What I needed was proof, so I took two steps. First, I removed Naissa to a place of safety in our home.'

'The risk being that Naissa might have been poisoned during the servants' mealtime—to prevent her remembering that it was Cassandra who handed her the poisoned chalice at the governor's reception?'

'Yes. And second, I kept a close eye on Paul at meal times here—waiting to catch Cassandra in the act of striking at her victim.'

'I can follow all of that,' said Cornelius, rubbing his chin and looking puzzled. 'But, if Cassandra was half the Falcon—then who is the other half?'

'That,' said Pop, 'is the mystery we must solve next. And Cassandra has ensured that we can never find out from her.'

Chapter 29

Before anyone could ask any more questions, a sergeant burst into the room with an urgent message for Commander Cornelius.

'An emergency has arisen,' said the commander as he read the note. 'I'm afraid you'll have to excuse me—my presence is required elsewhere.'

'What's happened, sir?' asked Captain Metellus.

'There's trouble at the *Delirium Tremens*.'

'What sort of trouble?'

'The sort that leaves a dozen people dead.'

'This news interests me greatly,' said Pop. 'May I accompany you?'

'Why yes, of course—if you wish.'

Commander Cornelius, Captain Metellus, Pop and I travelled to the scene in Cornelius's official car.

As we sped through the city streets, siren wailing, I asked Pop, 'Who killed Mr Cairo? Would that have been Cassandra?'

'I think not,' he replied. 'The other half of the Falcon—the organising half—would have made contact with Cairo, would subsequently have been approached for blackmail by that Egyptian businessman, and would then have murdered him.'

'It's unfortunate,' said Captain Metellus, 'that Cassandra committed suicide before she could be compelled to name her partner in "Falcon Incorporated".'

'It is unfortunate,' agreed Pop. 'I had not foreseen that possibility, and I blame myself for not taking precautions to prevent it.'

'At least,' I said, 'our problem is now halved. Cassandra's death, in effect, cuts off the Falcon's right hand. All that remains is to identify the other half of the assassination squad.'

'True,' said Pop. 'But unfortunately it is the more dangerous half of the Falcon that is still at large and, unless I miss my guess, frantic for revenge. In the "head" of the Falcon—the planning and organising half of the team—lies all that is most ingenious and most malicious.'

'I fear the consequences if we fail,' said Cornelius grimly.

'Be of good cheer,' Pop responded. 'Solomon says: "There is no future for the evil man—the lamp of the wicked will be put out".'

The car came to a halt in Wharf Street and we all piled out. Even in broad daylight the narrow alley in which the *Delirium Tremens* was located was drowned in deep shadows.

We had to negotiate our way around piles of garbage that littered the cobblestones, and the shadows and smells and dripping drains combined to create a mist of menace that rose like a nameless horror and made me shudder and glance over my shoulder.

Halfway down the alley, standing around the small

199

doorway of the bar was a cluster of officers from the city watch. They stepped aside and the four of us entered the damp and dingy tavern.

It was like stepping into a charnel house. Bodies lay scattered about, on the floor, collapsed across tables, propped against walls. Some of them had vomited before they died, and this added to the stench of the tavern that was now a tomb.

Dr Neronius Nausea was stepping gingerly amongst the corpses.

'My problem,' he explained as he greeted us, 'is knowing where to begin.'

'How did they die?' asked Cornelius.

'Poisoned. All poisoned.'

'What poison was used?' asked Pop.

'Ah, well. I don't like to make guesses, and the tests haven't been done yet.'

'Doctor,' said the Commander sternly, 'I don't care if it's a guess. Tell me what poison you suspect.'

'It's probably arsenic. But don't hold me to that until the autopsies have been done.'

The floor and the table tops were damp with the drinks the dying customers had spilled as they collapsed. The cards the poker players had held were scattered about amongst the debris.

'When did they die?' asked Captain Metellus.

'I don't like this,' complained Dr Nausea. 'I don't like it at all. I have barely arrived here, hardly begun my examinations, and I am being asked to make guesses about the poison used and the time of death.'

'Come now doctor,' said Cornelius. 'This is not in writing. No one is asking you to go on the record. But we need some sort of estimate. Did this carnage happen last night, for instance?'

'Good grief, no! The body temperature of these

corpses has barely begun to drop. And there's no sign of rigor mortis in any of them.'

'So most of them have died within the last hour, then?' said Pop.

'To be on the safe side, say within the last two hours,' muttered Nausea. 'Now I must keep moving. There's a massive amount of work here.'

'One last question,' said Pop. 'Did everyone who consumed the poison die?'

'Not at all. Those who were found ill but not dead have been taken to hospital.'

'Who is the proprietor of this hell hole?' asked Cornelius.

'It's a man named Felonius Caucus, sir,' replied Captain Metellus, 'a hard core criminal with a record as long as the governor's shopping list.'

'Where is he? He should be here answering questions.'

'He is one of those rushed to hospital,' explained Dr Nausea, 'and I would be inclined to put him on the critical list. It's touch and go at the moment for most of the survivors. And now, if you will excuse me Commander?' With that the portly little police surgeon returned to his work.

A few moments later the scene-of-crime officers arrived and began setting up lights and taking photographs. The blaze of the flood lamps and the bustle of activity lifted the atmosphere of gloom, but the lights also revealed the scope of the carnage that faced us. I counted thirteen corpses, and I may have missed some.

'Mass murder on this scale is rare,' said Captain Metellus. 'It's either the work of a homicidal maniac, or, more likely, a horrible accident.'

'For as many lunchtime drinkers as this to be

poisoned simultaneously,' said Pop, 'the arsenic must have been in the liquor.'

'But how did it get there, Pop?'

'Let's take a look and see,' he responded.

He led the way to the bar, which was little more than a simple wooden counter at the narrow end of the room. Stacked on shelves behind the bar were dozens of glasses, and at each end stood a wooden barrel.

Pop picked up a glass and half filled it from the tap in one of the barrels. He lifted the glass cautiously to his nose and sniffed.

'Rum,' he said, 'a rough, cheap rum.'

'Which is what I would expect in a waterfront bar like this,' said Metellus. 'This is the sort of place that would serve nothing but rum. And only the nastiest, cheapest sort of rum at that.'

'So we must assume then that some rat poison the proprietor was using has somehow got into the rum,' proposed Cornelius. 'You would agree?'

'Not necessarily,' said Pop.

'What other explanation could there be?'

'Revenge,' said Pop.

'Are you accusing Felonius Caucus of deliberately poisoning his own rum?'

'No, not that. Since he was himself poisoned, and is even now close to death, he is one of the victims in this case—not the villain.'

'Then who is?'

'Before answering that question, let us see how accessible these rum barrels are to a would-be mass murderer.'

'Well, for a start,' said Metellus, 'no one could have tampered with the barrels once they were sitting on the bar—they're in plain view of the whole room.'

'Granted,' said Pop. 'But where are the barrels kept

before they are placed on the bar?'

To find the answer to that question the four of us began a search of the premises.

Immediately behind the bar was a tiny kitchen which, judging from its state of cleanliness, specialised in serving 57 varieties of botulism. How any of the customers had survived until they got to the arsenic-laced rum I could not imagine.

From this kitchen a back door led out to a narrow lane, so narrow, in fact, that it was little more than a walkway between the buildings—like an open air corridor, no more than a metre wide. And here, stacked against the back wall of the *Delirium Tremens* was the rum supply: perhaps as many as two dozen of the small wooden barrels we had seen on the bar.

'Where does this laneway lead?' asked Pop.

'I'll check,' said Metellus, and he plunged into the gloomy shadows that filled the lane as it wound around the back walls of various buildings.

A few moments later he came back and announced that it opened into Wharf Street just a hundred yards north of the spot where we were standing.

'That, I think, is significant,' said Pop.

'In what way?' asked Cornelius.

'It shows that anyone could have made their way down this lane from Wharf Street, emptied a generous supply of white arsenic powder into one or more of the barrels, and departed again unobserved.'

'Yes, that would be easy,' agreed the Commander. 'But who would do such a thing? And why?'

'I agree with the Commander,' said Metellus. 'If this was a high class tavern I would guess that a deliberate mass poisoning might be done as punishment for refusal to pay protection money. But with a dive like the *Delirium Tremens* why would anyone bother?'

Pop responded by asking a question, 'What does the use of arsenic as a weapon of death suggest to you?'

'Well,' I volunteered, 'in the light of the case we are working on, it suggests the Falcon.'

'Precisely!' said Pop. 'The Falcon. Now desperate as well as malicious. On the one side his operation is under attack from the Fat Man—who had his fee stolen and the carrier of his fee killed. And on the other side he is pressed by us—who have now cost him his "right hand" as you put it a moment ago.'

'You think the Falcon did this?' asked Metellus skeptically.

'Perhaps you're getting just a little obsessed with this Falcon,' suggested Cornelius with a smile.

'Think!' said Pop sharply. 'Think about what has happened. I pointed out before that the Falcon must strike back at the Fat Man over the theft of his fee. He must take his revenge, or else the fear upon which his reputation is based is destroyed for ever. This bar, although operated by Felonious Caucus is actually owned by the Fat Man. We all know that. And it is mainly members of the Fat Man's gang who are the customers here—this tavern is notorious as their meeting place. With one single, bold stroke the Falcon has cut a swathe through the Fat Man's gang and closed down one of his centres of operations. An effective act of revenge for the theft of his fee, wouldn't you say?'

'Yes! Of course! That makes sense,' said Metellus.

'So this act of carnage is the Falcon's response to the Fat Man—a sort of *quid pro quo*?' I said.

Cornelius looked at me, his eyebrows raised in

surprise. 'I didn't know you spoke Italian, Sam,' he said.

As the four of us made our way back into the tavern I asked, 'What does this revenge by mass murder tell us about the Falcon's operations now?'

'It tells us,' said Pop, 'that he is desperate, and that his desperation is making him more homicidal and more dangerous than ever before.'

Chapter 30

The next hour was something of a blur. Cornelius ordered both barrels of rum standing on the bar to be taken to the Official Alchemist for analysis, and then left Captain Metellus in charge of the investigation at the tavern.

The Commander, Pop and I returned to the palace, and went straight up to Paul's rooms to report that the half of the Falcon that was still in business was still active—and more dangerous than ever.

With Pop in deep conversation with Paul I decided to return to our office to find something to occupy my mind. The sheer horror of the Falcon's capacity for death was depressing me, and only activity, I knew, would shake off the feeling that a cloud of great evil hung over the city of Caesarea.

For the same reason I wanted to walk rather than catch a bus. I needed fresh air and sunlight to clear the stench of death out of my nostrils.

Tim had some letters to post for Paul, and he

offered to walk with me as far as the Forum.

The street in which the palace stood was a broad, tree-lined avenue. I breathed the fresh, clean air deep into my lungs, and turning to Tim I said, 'Investigating the Falcon is like handling garbage—I feel as though I need a shower afterwards to wash away the grime and the smell.

'I've always said that I hate studying law, but after seeing that mass poisoning the thought of sitting in a sunny lecture theatre, nodding off to sleep while some professor drones on from the lectern seems most attractive.'

We walked on in silence for a short while, and then I said, 'Actually, I have an important decision to make about my law studies.'

'Tell me about it,' said Tim.

'Well, it's just that a possible job offer has bobbed up—a very attractive offer as it happens. There is nothing I would like more than to throw away the law books and take the job. But there is part of me that still feels unsure about it.'

'Choices are hard to make. But it's by our choices that we live.'

'Yeah,' I said ruefully, 'We have to live with the consequences. At least our bad choices get buried with us.'

'Are you sure?' said Tim. 'What about the Big Choice that everyone has to face in one form or another.'

'Which choice—exactly—are we talking about?'

'The choice about our basic life posture—about how we live.'

'How we live is mostly a matter of just muddling through: the tracks are not that clear cut!'

'Granted. But it is possible to cut through the muddle—to bring the picture into focus so to speak—and when you do that, you can see that in the end there are really only two ways to live.'

'There are lots of different ways to live! There are probably as many different ways to live as there are people in the world.'

'In a sense you're quite right. But what I'm saying is that when you look at all the different ways people live, they really fall into only two categories. It's as though there are two roads, and everyone's individual life track—however much it wanders about—leads onto one or other of those two roads.'

'Well, what two ways are there?'

'Our way or God's way. That's all there is in the end!'

I listened in silence to Tim's words.

'So,' he continued, 'which of these is the way you want to live?'

'I don't know. I'm being honest with you, Tim. Put like that I really don't know. It's too big a choice. I think I'm frightened of losing control of my life. And I'm worried about what I'll miss out on. I'm just not ready to choose. Not now. Perhaps later, but not now.'

By this time we had reached the Forum so I turned towards our office and Tim headed off to post his letters.

When I arrived Zimri seemed relieved to see me.

'Ah, Mr Samuel,' he said, 'I'm glad you've come. This urgent message has just arrived for you by courier.'

He handed me an envelope with my name and the word 'urgent' in big black letters on the front. I tore it open and read this message:

The game's afoot! The job is yours. Come to the

Continental Detective Agency office the moment you receive this message.

(signed) Publius Camillus.

That was what I had been waiting for!

On reading that message everything else went straight out of my head.

'Zimri,' I said, 'I have to go out. Tell Pop I may be some time.'

And with that I was bounding down the stairs towards my new life of adventure as a Private Eye.

Chapter 31

It was late in the afternoon, and the shadows were lengthening, as I hurried across town.

I took a short cut through the cinema district, the gaudy advertising posters flashing past my eyes as I hurried on. One theatre, I noticed, was screening a festival of Steve Reeves gladiator movies. Well, I wouldn't be going to see those: I hate documentaries.

Another theatre was showing a triple bill of three spectacular epics: *Spartan Wars* and its two sequels *The Roman Empire Strikes Back* and *Return of the Gauls*. Next door they were screening a slapstick comedy: *Gladiator Academy IV*.

I pushed past the crowds that were gathering around the foyers of the movie-houses, and hurried on through the cinema district.

Soon I was walking quickly through the narrow, dark alleys on the harbour side of the Forum. It was that time in the evening when all the honest folk were sitting down to eat with their friends and families, in the houses, cafes, and coffee shops of Caesarea.

The lanes and alleys I hurried through, as I headed towards the waterfront district, were deserted, dark, gloomy and forbidding.

At length I came to the alley in which were located the offices of the Continental Detective Agency. I plunged into the doorway of the narrow tenement building, intending to bound up the stairs to the second floor office, when I found my way barred by four broad-shouldered, leather-jacketed young men.

'You going somewhere?' one of them sneered.

'In a hurry are you?' added a second.

The remaining two were silent, and in the darkness of the doorway I could see none of their faces.

Before I knew what was happening the one in the centre landed his fist heavily in my midriff. Suddenly I was bent double, desperately trying to suck in air.

'I said,' he grunted, 'are you going somewhere?'

Seeing his shoulder move as he drew back to throw another punch I used the last few centimetres of air in my lungs to gasp out, 'Upstairs. . . detective. . . agency. . .'

'They're closed,' said another of the young men on my right, 'closed permanently.'

By now my wind was starting to return, and I let go of my aching mid section and straightened up. 'I've got an appointment,' I said.

'It's been cancelled,' said the one on my right.

'What's happened?' I asked, trying to sound as innocent as possible. In reply, there was a chorus of response from all of them:

'They've shut up shop.'

'And moved out of town.'

'Couldn't pay their bills.'

'So they ain't here any more.'

'Uh huh, I see,' I said. 'Well, there's no point in my

hanging around then,' and I turned to go. As I did so the four young hoodlums drew back into the shadows and resumed their waiting position.

I took a step away from the door, and, when I was certain that they were convinced I was leaving, I spun around and flung myself at them.

There were four of them and one of me, but I had caught them by surprise. My boot collected a shin and one of them pulled back, squealing with pain. I found two heads and banged them together. Hard. They made a satisfyingly solid impact. And it gave me great pleasure to thrust my fist into the stomach of the one who had punched me, and see him double up as I had.

But with my surprise advantage gone, the weight of numbers began to tell. I took a heavy punch to the side of the head and staggered back. Then I had fists and boots coming at me faster than I could move. Several hard kidney punches brought me to the ground.

They were about to lay into me seriously and break a few ribs when I became aware of a wild disturbance and cries of alarm among my attackers. Someone else had joined the fight—on my side. I struggled to my feet and began throwing punches again.

There were two of us fighting side by side in the darkness, and the four young hoodlums didn't like those odds so much. After another two or three bruising minutes, they turned and fled.

I collapsed onto the bottom step, aware of a trickle of warm blood running down the side of my face, aware too of sharp aches and throbbing pains all over my body. I turned to see who my rescuer might be, and in the dim light of a street lamp could make out a rugged profile.

'Dash!' I said. 'It's you!'

'You were expecting Julius Caesar maybe? Come

on up to the office and we'll get you cleaned up,' he said, taking my arm and helping me to my feet.

Upstairs he dabbed iodine onto my wounds while I flinched and grunted out 'Ah! Ooo! Ouch! That hurts!' and similar expressions of interest in the proceedings.

'That should do you,' said Dash at length. 'I don't think you're going to die. Here, join me in a glass of the office brandy. Purely for medicinal reasons of course.'

I accepted the glass he held out, and then asked, 'What was that all about?'

'I've no idea,' said Dash calmly, apparently quite undisturbed by the whole incident. 'It's just something that goes with the territory. We make a lot of enemies in this business.'

'But aren't you even interested in who they were, and what they were up to?'

'I know who they were: a bunch of petty hoods. And I know what they were up to: trying to put the frighteners on the Continental Detective Agency. I don't much care which bunch of hoods they were, or why we've upset them. All that matters is they've failed.'

'But. . .'

'This is a tough business we are in, Sam. You'll find that we run into heavy boys like that quite often. Now, finish your brandy, we have somewhere to go.'

A thrill of excitement and anticipation ran down my spine when Dash talked about this tough business that 'we are in'—to be accepted by Dash as his partner was an ambition I had harboured since high school.

'I got a message to come here,' I explained, 'to meet Camillus. He's not here?'

'He sent me to pick you up. He's out on the yacht. So finish up that brandy and we'll get going.'

I swallowed down the last of the brandy in one gulp,

recovered from my fit of coughing and spluttering, and said, 'okay—let's go.'

Dash locked up the office and led the way downstairs, through the few streets that stood between the office and the docks of Caesarea harbour, past several closed and locked warehouses, and out onto a long, narrow timber wharf. At the end were steps leading down to the water's edge, and bouncing on the small waves, at the end of the steps, was a power boat.

The waves lapped in a desultory and oily fashion against the piers of the wharf as we stepped into the boat and Dash untied the painter.

As the boat drifted away from the steps on the slow, sludgy swell that rippled across the harbour, Dash took his seat behind the wheel and I lowered myself into the seat beside him. He switched on the electric starter and kicked over the powerful engine in the stern. After one false start, that ended in an uncertain splutter, the engine caught and started to rumble with a low, throaty roar.

Dash eased open the throttle and steered a careful path between the buoys and pleasure craft moored around the wharf. When we were in more open water he opened up the power and we thundered across the width of Caesarea's great harbour, skipping and bouncing over the low swell that rippled in from the harbour mouth.

The movement of the boat turned the still, evening air into a sharp, salty breeze that whipped through our hair.

'There's the yacht,' yelled Dash over the roar of the engine, after we had been travelling for some minutes. 'Just ahead of us there.'

Peering ahead into the wind I could make out the vessel we were heading towards. The 'yacht' was, in fact, a huge motor cruiser: fifty metres of expensive, gleaming white luxury. This, I thought, is what the Roman nobility regard as comfortable boating.

Dash throttled off and let our boat drift under its own momentum the last dozen metres to the 'yacht'. A few moments later we bumped gently against the side and Dash grabbed a rope that dangled down from a bollard on the deck, apparently in anticipation of our arrival. He secured our boat to this rope and then called out, 'Ahoy! Ahoy aboard there!'

In response, a moment later, the face of Publius Camillus peered at us over the railing.

'That you Dash?' he called as he squinted into the darkness.

'It's me. And I've got Sam with me.'

'Excellent. Stand by.'

A moment later a rope ladder uncurled from the deck, its end flopping almost on to our laps.

I grabbed the swaying ladder and, groping carefully for each shifting hand- and foot-hold, clambered to the top.

On the deck Camillus nodded to me in his rather superior, patrician way. 'Welcome aboard, Sam,' he said, 'and welcome to the team.'

When Dash joined us Camillus asked, 'No trouble?'

'Nothing major,' replied Dash.

'Fine,' said his boss. 'Follow me and we'll have some refreshments. We need to fuel up for the night ahead of us.'

What night ahead of us? I wondered. What was Camillus planning? And what was my role in his plans?

Chapter 32

The cabin Camillus led us into was, quite clearly, only one of many on the floating palace he called his yacht. This particular cabin—flooded with a warm, yellow light—might have been a navigator's office. Comfortable leather chairs surrounded a large, central table. Maps showing the whole of the Mediterranean were pinned to the walls, and other rolled up maps were stacked in the corners of the cabin.

On this occasion the table was occupied not by maps but by a large picnic basket.

Moments later the table was covered with fresh crusty bread rolls, cold chicken, caviar, smoked salmon, paté, cheeses, fresh fruit, and a large bottle of champagne.

'Just a little snack,' said Camillus, gesturing modestly at the feast before us. 'Tuck in, and enjoy yourselves.'

Dash and I needed no further invitation—it's strange how hungry fighting can make you.

The next hour or more was principally occupied

with the serious business of eating and conversation was of the occasional and jovial kind that accompanies a delicious meal.

At last, having succeeded in demolishing the contents of the basket, we eased our chairs back and raised our glasses to toast what Camillus called "the adventure the night has in store for us".

'And what adventure might that be?' I asked.

'You haven't briefed him yet?' enquired Camillus, addressing Dash.

'No,' said Dash, 'I thought you'd prefer to do that yourself.'

'Quite right, quite right—so I would.'

Camillus took a deep breath and began to explain.

'You will understand, Sam,' he began, 'that in the detective trade we are asked to tackle a very wide range of tasks. Protection and security operations, for example, missing persons, and that grubby business— divorce evidence. One of our most important areas of activity is debt recovery. Imagine that a businessman is owed a certain sum of money but no payment is forthcoming. When his patience finally gives out it is quite likely that he will come to the Continental Detective Agency to collect on his behalf.'

'But what about the courts?' I asked.

'What do you mean "what about the courts"?' snapped Camillus.

'I mean—wouldn't the businessman's first step be to apply for a court order requiring prompt payment of the debt?'

'Oh, yes, I see what you mean. And the answer is— yes, of course that happens. But how is the debt, recognised by the court order, to be collected if the debtor still refuses to pay?'

'Can't the sheriff's officers impound the debtor's

property?'

'Yes they can. That is what the law says should happen. And what you are doing, young Sam, is reciting what you have learned in your legal text books. But the world is not a legal text book, and things don't happen just as they should.'

'I don't understand.'

'Then I will explain. Suppose the debtor becomes absolutely determined not to pay his debt. In that case he will hide his assets so that there is nothing of significant value for the sheriff's officers to seize. What do your text books tell you to do then?'

'Well. . . actually. . . the text books don't deal with that contingency.'

'Of course they don't! Because they can't! That is where the law falls flat on its pompous face! And that is when some extra-legal force has to come in and sort out the mess. That's us. In my example the businessman would come to the Continental Detective Agency with his problem. And I should add that Dash here has quite a reputation in Caesarea as a forceful and persuasive debt collector.'

Dash chuckled modestly and looked down into his drink. He was clearly proud of his reputation, but it didn't strike me as anything to be particularly proud of.

'Our task tonight,' said Camillus, 'is a debt collection task.'

'Who are we collecting from?' I asked.

'All you need to know is that you are part of the Continental Agency's task force tonight on what will be a difficult, and possibly dangerous, operation. Do well tonight and you join us permanently as a detective. Are you with us or not?'

'Oh, I'm with you all right!' I said.

'Fine. I will be leading the team personally, but our expedition cannot begin until much later tonight. So, until then Sam, I suggest that you make yourself at home. Explore the yacht if you wish. Dash, you have the freedom of the liquor cabinet—but make sure you are sober when I need you tonight. I'm going to my cabin, and I'll see you two later.'

With that Camillus left us.

Dash found a bottle of whisky, a soda syphon, and a bucket of crushed ice. With these beside him he seemed in need of no other companions, so I decided to accept Camillus's invitation, and I set off to explore all three decks of this giant motor cruiser.

Starting with the open deck at the aft of the vessel I began my tour of inspection. Secured in derricks at the aft railing was a small skiff. Raising its canvas covering I peered inside and discovered that it contained a surprisingly large in-board motor. This innocent looking skiff, I decided, would be as fast across the water as the speed boat.

Near the bow I found some life buoys that told me the name of the vessel I was on: *M.V. Victorius* was painted on each one. Standing in the bow I looked back towards Caesarea harbour.

The town centre showed up as a thick cluster of twinkling lights, like candles on a distant birthday cake. Each of those lights represented a room—warm and snug, and filled with people, and companionship, and laughter. And for the first time I regretted where I was and what I was doing. A cold hand clutched my heart as I contemplated the mysterious adventure to which I was committed that night.

Putting such thoughts out of my mind, I walked down a companionway to explore the bowels of the *Victorius*.

219

The companionway opened into a corridor that ran the length of the ship. I tried one or two of the doors that opened off it, and found opulent and luxurious sleeping accommodation behind each one. At the end of this corridor another companionway took me to a lower level.

Down here I could hear the engines ticking over quietly. At the end of a much shorter corridor was a closed door marked "engine room". Other doors opened into the galley and various storage lockers.

I opened one door and found myself face to face with four of the ugliest, toughest looking sailors I've ever seen in my life. They were seated around a small table playing cards. At the sound of the door opening all four looked up from their game and stared at me.

'I'm... I'm sorry...' I stuttered and hurriedly closed the door again.

I went back up to the cabin where we had eaten our meal. Dash was nowhere to be seen. Perhaps he had taken his drink out into the cool ocean air on the aft deck. Or perhaps he had gone somewhere to confer with Camillus.

I lay down on the bunk that was fixed to the bulkhead, and, to my own surprise, dozed off to sleep. The next thing I knew my shoulder was being shaken vigorously.

'Come on sleeping beauty,' said Dash, 'It's midnight, time to go.'

Chapter 33

Camillus led the way to the speed boat still moored at the side of the *Victorius*. All three of us clambered down the swaying rope ladder, Dash settled himself at the controls and soon we were bouncing across Caesarea harbour towards what was, for me, still an unknown destination.

Then, once we were through the maze of moored ships, Dash eased the throttle open a little further and steered towards the furthest end of the harbour.

'Not too much throttle,' muttered Camillus. 'We don't want to be heard.'

Five minutes later he turned off the engine and we drifted the last dozen metres to the shore. The keel bumped against the gently sloping sandy bottom of the bay.

'Everybody out,' ordered Camillus, 'and pull the boat up onto the beach.'

When the boat was on the dry sand of the beach Dash tied the painter to a convenient rock, and turned to Camillus to take the lead.

'This way,' said the head of the Continental Detective Agency.

Dash and I followed to a point where the sandy beach ended and a rocky outcrop commenced. Clambering over these rocks we came to what looked like the entrance to a large cave.

'In here,' said Camillus, and we followed him into the cave mouth.

Publius Camillus pulled a small flashlight out of his pocket and continued to lead the way.

Along the centre of the floor of the cave trickled a small, foul smelling stream which we were careful to avoid. Stumbling I reached out to steady myself against the wall, and was startled by how smooth and perfectly round it was. Then I realised we had entered one of the giant outlet pipes of Caesarea's underground sewers.

The tunnel ahead of us wound onwards, with tributaries joining it at regular intervals. Several times we came to major junction points, where three or four of the large pipes came together. At these Camillus would turn to Dash and ask, 'Which way?' Without hesitation Dash would indicate and we would resume our rapid walking.

I remembered being told that smugglers, and other Caesarean criminals, regularly used these tunnels as a kind of underground highway system, and I realised that Dash must have become familiar with this network through his work as a detective, tracking down those smugglers.

After some time the tunnel floor began to slope upwards, and I understood that we must now be somewhere underneath the hills that rose to the east of the city.

At length the large tunnel that had been our highway came to an end, and we entered a much smaller one that we had to stoop to pass through. It was at this point I came to regret the fact that these tunnels actually functioned as sewers. In the larger tunnel it had been easy to keep my feet out of the foul-smelling stream that trickled down the middle, but in the smaller tunnel this was much harder, and occasionally I would stumble and my feet splash in something I would rather not think about.

Soon this smaller tunnel too began to slope, and this time quite steeply. Still we walked on, all three of us in a bent and stooped posture. As we continued I was pleased to note that the tunnel was becoming drier, and less offensive.

'Hold on,' said Dash, eventually, 'it's about here somewhere.'

Camillus flashed his light around the ceiling of the sewer. 'I can't see it.'

'A little further then,' replied Dash. 'It can't be far.'

We now proceeded slowly, Camillus examining the roof over our heads every few steps.

'There!' said Dash, 'Just ahead—I can see it.'

'Ah yes,' said Camillus, turning his light in the direction indicated by Dash. 'Are you sure this is the one?'

'Trust me,' said Dash. 'I know what I'm doing. This is the place.'

The flashlight was shining on a circular steel plate in the roof of the sewer: a manhole cover.

Standing directly underneath, and placing his palms firmly against the cover, Dash straightened up, and with a grunt of effort lifted the steel cover from its resting place.

'Here—Sam—give me a hand,' he grunted.

I hurried to his side and helped to push the manhole cover to one side. Dash then reached up, grabbed the sides of the now open hole with his hands, and pulled himself up. Camillus followed him, and I came last.

When I emerged into the sweet-smelling fresh night air I found that we were in a narrow side street. Immediately behind us was a brick wall, while directly opposite were the backs of a row of houses, all in darkness, the inhabitants, I had no doubt, comfortably in their beds and sound asleep.

'Give me a hand,' said Dash, indicating that we should move the manhole cover back into place.

'Quiet, you two!' hissed Camillus. 'Are you trying to wake the entire neighbourhood!'

His reprimand was uncalled for. It was just the sound of his nerves snapping.

The cover back in place, we brushed off our hands and knees, and I wiped my shoes on the long grass that stood at the foot of the high brick wall.

I wondered which of the houses was our target. I was surprised when Camillus turned his dimmed flashlight on the brick wall and said, 'This is where we are going.'

'Give me a leg up, Sam,' said Dash.

I put my back against the wall, Dash placed one foot in my hands, and with a grunt of effort, pushed himself up onto the top of the wall.

I braced myself again, to give Camillus a lift. Then they pulled as I jumped, and the next moment I was balancing between them on top of a wall no more than a foot wide. Ahead of us, inside the wall, were rolling lawns studded with bushes. Some distance away, behind a row of trees, I could dimly discern the outline of a large house—a mansion, no less.

'That,' whispered Camillus, 'is our target.'

'Let's get going,' I whispered in reply. My nerves were on edge, and I was anxious for all this to be over.

'Wait,' said Camillus, placing a restraining hand on my arm. I turned and looked at the Roman. The cold, pale light of the quarter moon caught his beaky profile, giving him a savage predatory look.

Camillus dug deep into one of his pockets and pulled out a strange-looking gun. It was a 9-millimetre Beretta double-action semi-automatic pistol. The strange appearance was caused by the heavy silencer fitted to the barrel.

'Okay,' said Camillus, breathing heavily, 'now!'

All three of us lept to the ground simultaneously.

'Freeze,' hissed Dash. 'Listen!'

I listened, but couldn't hear anything. I was about to turn to Dash and complain when a low rustling sound alerted me to the approach of someone—or something.

Suddenly two low, dark shapes shot like torpedoes across the law towards us. Camillus dropped to a crouching position and raised the pistol in both hands. Aiming carefully he squeezed the trigger once, and then, shifting slightly, a second time.

Each shot made the sinister spitting noise of a silenced pistol. Each of the dark shapes dropped dead in its tracks.

'Good shooting,' I whispered.

'Let's check,' said Camillus rising to his feet.

We walked over to the dark motionless shapes. They were dogs—large, black dogs with vicious looking teeth. Both were dead.

'Why didn't they bark?' I asked.

'He had them de-barked,' said Dash. 'He wanted them to kill intruders, not warn them.'

I didn't ask who "he" was, since I was certain I wouldn't be told.

'Right,' said Camillus. 'Move on. Quietly.'

We crept forward over the rolling lawn, and through

the trees towards the mansion.

When we came to the edge of the belt of trees we stopped again.

'Will there be any guards?' asked Camillus.

'Not at night,' said Dash. 'Just the dogs and the alarm system.'

Following Dash's lead we circled around the back of the building to what I took to be a kitchen door.

'Shine the light up there,' said Dash, pointing at the top right hand corner of the door post, as he produced a screwdriver and a pair of pliers.

Working under the dim light held by Camillus, Dash scratched at the paintwork of the doorpost.

'Gently, gently,' he whispered to himself. 'Mustn't break the circuit. There it is!'

His probing had revealed a thick wire, buried in a groove in the timber doorpost, and hidden under a heavy coat of paint. Using the point of the screwdriver Dash eased the wire out of its groove, then gripped it firmly in the jaws of the pliers, and with a sharp snap cut it through.

Then Dash turned to Camillus and me and said quietly, with a smile on his face, 'Gentlemen—shall we step inside?'

Chapter 34

Dash slipped the screwdriver and pliers into one pocket, and fished a set of skeleton keys out of another.

For a minute or two he quietly jiggled these in the door lock, then there was a firm click, he turned the knob, the door swung open, and he stood back to let his boss lead the way into the dark house.

I was the last to enter, and when I did so I found we were in some kind of pantry; it was a small room, the walls were lined with shelves and the shelves stacked with food.

'Let me borrow the light for a moment,' said Dash, and, taking the offered flashlight from Camillus's hand, he searched the walls.

Within a minute he found what he was looking for—an electrical switch box. Opening this he turned off all the switches *and* removed the fuses.

'Now,' he said, as he handed the flashlight back to Camillus, 'we can be certain of being undisturbed.'

Camillus took the lead again, and opened the pantry door onto a dark corridor. We clustered in the doorway for a moment while Camillus got his bearings.

'The office is to the right?' he whispered to Dash.

'Yes—down that way,' was the softly breathed reply.

Before going any further Camillus produced, from a deep jacket pocket, several slender canisters. He ripped a pull-tab from the top of one of these and instantly thick grey smoke began to pour out. He rolled the smoking canister down the corridor to the left and then set off to the right, whispering 'Follow me!' over his shoulder as he did so.

We worked our way silently down the corridor, which seemed to make many unexpected turns as it wove its way down the length of the house.

Coming to a large door on our left Camillus paused for a moment. 'What's in here?' he asked.

Dash concentrated for a moment and then replied, 'A formal dining room.'

Camillus eased open the door, pulled the tab on another of the canisters, and rolled it into the room as thick smoke began to appear.

We continued down the dark corridor, our only light being the dim silvery moonlight that crept in through a distant window.

My heart almost exploded with fear when a sharp beeping sound started somewhere behind us in the darkness.

'I thought you disabled that!' I said accusingly to Dash.

'That's not the burglar alarm. It's the fire alarm, set off by the smoke detector,' he snapped.

'But... but you pulled out all the fuses... didn't you?'

'It's on a separate circuit. Now shut up, Sam, and keep moving,' Dash snarled, turning me around and pushing me roughly in the middle of the back.

Another few steps brought us to a heavy wooden

door on our right.

'This must be the one,' said Camillus.

'That's it,' confirmed Dash.

'Break it in!' commanded the Roman.

'Stand back,' warned Dash.

Camillus and I withdrew a few steps, Dash drew back a short distance and then kicked hard at the lock with the heavily booted sole of his foot. The door frame gave with a crunch of splintering timber, and a moment later we were inside.

The room appeared to be, from what I could see in that dim moonlight, a large and luxurious office.

'Sam,' growled Camillus, 'set this going outside the door, and then jam the door closed behind us.' And he handed me the last of his canisters. I ripped off the pull-tab as I had seen him do, and rolled the now smoking canister into the hallway behind us. Then I dragged up some heavy chairs which I jammed hard against the closed door as a substitute for the broken lock and shattered door frame.

Voices could now be heard throughout the house. The fire alarm sounded louder—perhaps a second alarm had now joined the first—and cries of 'Fire! Fire!' could be heard.

Camillus and Dash ignored all this, and working by flashlight made their way to a large wall-safe.

Camillus handed the flashlight to Dash, and settled down to work on the safe. Hanging around his neck, underneath his jacket, he had a stethoscope. This he applied to the safe door so that he could hear the tumblers fall into place as he delicately manipulated the dial that worked the combination.

Camillus and Dash were concentrating intensely on breaking into the safe, but I was, for the moment, unoccupied. As I wandered idly around the office I had a shock of recognition: this was a room that I vaguely knew. I had been here before. But when? And what room was it?

Then in a blinding flash I knew! And, stunned by my discovery, I blurted it out loud: 'This is the Fat Man's office! This is his house!'

For a moment Camillus stopped his concentrated work to turn and stare at me. 'So what!'

'Is it the Fat Man who owes you money?' I asked.

'Of course it is!' snapped Camillus. 'And it's also none of your business! You are my employee and you do what you are told. Shut up. Stand guard at the door. Keep an ear on what's happening. Those are your orders.' With that the Roman nobleman turned back to working on the safe door.

Feeling dazed, confused and unsure of myself, I walked back towards the office door. Outside, in the corridor, there were running footsteps and alarmed voices. Cries of panic were now ringing out from every part of the house. In the distance the siren of an approaching fire engine could be heard .

'Hurry up,' urged Dash.

'Shut up and let me get on with it,' said Camillus.

Soon there was a heavy banging against the office door as the occupants of the house tried to get in to rescue their valuables from the flames they imagined were about to engulf them.

'Sam—move more furniture against that door!' yelled Dash. And in my dazed state I could do nothing except obey. I dragged a heavy sofa across the carpet and propped it up to support the chairs that were jamming the door closed.

The hammering grew louder and more insistent, and still Camillus worked with feverish fingers on the wall safe, spinning the dials, listening for the tumblers, and trying to make the combination fall into place and open the lock.

The sounds in the corridor changed from panic to an orderly busy-ness. The fire brigade had arrived, and a platoon of city watch officers with them by the sound of it.

Most of the voices were indistinguishable in the hubbub, but one young voice rose clearly above the rest. 'Sir, sir, take a look at this canister.'

Dash and Camillus stopped and looked at each other. Within a minute, they knew, their deception would be penetrated, and all efforts would concentrate on getting the office door open.

'We've got to get out!' said Dash.

'Go if you want to,' said Camillus. 'I'm not leaving without the money.'

Dash didn't stir, he kept holding the flashlight for his boss, but he looked alarmed and uneasy.

Soon the banging on the office door became a heavy, regular battering, and the door began to move slowly inwards.

'Got it!' cried Camillus as the safe door flew open.

Out of the safe he clawed thick bundles of cash, which he stuffed into his deep jacket pockets. As he did so Dash ran to the window, opened it, and began climbing out. Camillus stuffed his pockets until they bulged, and then followed Dash to the window.

'Come on, Sam!' he yelled at me as he ran.

I had been frozen to the spot by fear and confusion, and his words had a defrosting effect. I was about to run after Camillus when the door behind me shattered open, and a crowd of figures burst into the room.

Among them were faces I recognised: there was Captain Metullus of the city watch, Commander Cornelius, and, standing right in the middle, my father!

I looked at the face of Ben Bartholomew, lawyer, detective, and father, and the pain I saw written there stabbed clear through me.

'Pop!' I said.

Then a voice rang out clearly from the other side of the room. 'Sam—come quickly!'

It was Camillus. He was at the window now, beckoning me to join him. He grabbed a thick wad of money from his pocket and held it up. 'Look what's waiting for you, Sam! More money than you ever dreamed of. Come on!'

I glanced back towards Pop.

'Sam. . .' was all he said. And as he said it he held out his hand.

At that moment, time stood still. It was as though every clock in the world was frozen.

And in that frozen moment, a moment not of time but of eternity, I saw clearly the choice I was facing.

Camillus was offering me money, and, no doubt, everything that money could buy. His life was symbolised by the luxurious motor cruiser that was waiting in the harbour. I could feel the tug of the appeal of self indulgence, of the satisfaction of every earthly desire.

But I hesitated.

Even though Camillus was offering me the fulfilment of ambitions I had nurtured for years, I hesitated.

Was Camillus really offering me freedom, pleasure and self indulgence? Or was he asking me to enrol in his service, to take his orders?

I looked back at Pop, and saw everything he represented to me: a life not concerned with self, and self's priorities, but with God and God's priorities. I knew then that I was facing the choice that Tim had talked to me about. . . when? Only the previous afternoon? It seemed like an age ago.

In that frozen moment in time I closed my eyes and I prayed. I asked God to do what I could never do myself—to *change* me, so that I would not do what *I* wanted but what *he* wanted, so that I could learn to live his way.

An awful weight rolled away. And, in that moment, I felt more freedom than I had ever felt in my life before.

The moment ended. The clocks ticked again. Eternity receded and time took over.

'Sam!' yelled Camillus.

I turned my back on him, and in a few strides was at my father's side.

Pop threw his arms around me and gave me a hug. 'Sam, you have escaped,' he said, 'from the claws of the Falcon.'

And he pointed at the fleeing figure of Camillus.

Chapter 35

My head was spinning. I wanted to say something, but the words wouldn't come. My emotions were a whirlpool: I felt simultaneously betrayed by Camillus and Dash, and secure in my father's acceptance.

I had been confronted by a decision I thought I could delay indefinitely, and I had discovered how dangerous delay can be.

And then there was the startling announcement that Pop had just made. Startling to me at least. Camillus? The Falcon? I just didn't understand.

'There'll be time enough for explanations later,' said Pop. 'But first, please explain how you came to be here.'

So I did. I told Pop, Cornelius and Metellus about the job offer that Camillus had made, about my response, and about the surprising nature of what the job turned out to be.

'I think I can say officially,' said Cornelius with a glance at Captain Metellus, 'that you have clearly been the victim of a deception. As a result, you will not be facing any criminal charges over the events of this night.'

Criminal charges? Until the commander said the words out loud, it had not even occurred to me that I had, unwittingly, assisted at a house breaking and robbery.

'I didn't. . .' I started to explain lamely. But I couldn't continue: I knew I had been a complete idiot.

'Don't be too hard on yourself,' said Pop, responding to the expression on my face. 'There was no reason for you to assume the job offer was anything but genuine, and then you were kept in the dark until it was too late for you to pull back.'

Cornelius nodded in agreement.

It was nice of them, but I still felt like an idiot.

'If you'll excuse me,' said Captain Metellus as he turned to leave us, 'I'll check on how the search is going.'

'What a fool,' I said, 'not to see what was really going on.'

'Well the logic of the universe functions much as it has always functioned,' said Pop. 'It is only by the grace of God that most of us manage to see beneath the surface, and understand what's really going on.'

Cornelius just slapped me heartily on the shoulder, and said, 'I'm glad that you've come through it unscathed anyhow, young Sam.'

'How come you people arrived with the fire brigade?' I asked.

'Ben alerted us to the probability that the Falcon would seek some sort of further revenge against the Fat Man, and we were prepared to respond quickly to any call from this house.'

'Where is the Fat Man, by the way?' I asked.

'Out on his front lawn, wrapped up in a blanket and

full of injured pride,' said Pop.

'And we are using the opportunity to do a little searching,' added Cornelius. 'Already my men have turned up evidence that links the Fat Man to several recent crimes. I suspect that at this stage he has a rather confined future facing him.'

At that moment Metellus hurried back into the room to report to the Commander. 'We can't find them anywhere. Both Publius Camillus and the other man have vanished.'

'The sewer!' I burst out. 'That's where they will have gone.'

'Show us,' said Metellus, and I set off at a run, the others at my heels, to the sewer manhole in the side street that was, I was certain, the escape route they had taken.

'This is the way we came,' I said, pointing at the manhole cover in the middle of the road.

'You two men—shift that cover,' ordered Metellus.

As soon as the cover was lifted I dropped down into the sewer, calling out as I did so, 'Come on—I'll show you the way.'

Soon I was leading a party that included a number of city watch officers, Commander Cornelius, and Pop, in a stooped run down the narrow sewer. I stumbled once, and one of the officers handed me his powerful flashlight. With that broad beam of light showing the way we travelled even faster.

Before long we reached the main sewer and were able to stand erect. The city watch officers spread out in a line, as the pursuit continued at a cracking pace. The sound of running feet and shouted commands echoed around us as we moved through the vast underground tunnel.

Navigating proved not to be a problem. At each

junction point I just had to keep the party moving in the direction the narrow stream in the middle of the conduit was flowing—downhill, towards the harbour.

After some time I spotted, a long way ahead of us, the dim gleam of a small flashlight.

'There they are!' I yelled.

An officer dropped into a crouching position and fired twice, in the direction of the light, then we hurried on, past another major junction, to the point where we had glimpsed the light.

One of the leading younger officers now called back over his shoulder, 'There's someone here.'

The young officer was crouching over a fallen figure. It was Dash, sprawled out across the floor of the sewer, blood pumping from a bullet wound to his chest.

At first I thought he was dead, but when I bent over, and spoke his name, his eyes opened.

'Sam. . .' he said feebly.

'Don't try to talk. We'll have an ambulance officer here soon.'

'No point. . . far too late,' he stopped, licked his lips and took a deep breath.

'Did you know?' I asked. 'Did you know that Camillus was the Falcon?'

'No. . . I hadn't figured it out,' he said, with a gurgling sound in his throat. Dash coughed several times, took a deep breath, and spoke again, 'Always thought I was such a great detective. . . so did you. . . but he had me fooled.'

'Rest your head back Dash,' I insisted. 'Help will be here soon.'

'Help. . . will be too late. . . you know that, Sam,' he coughed blood as he spoke.

His eyes closed and I thought he had gone, so I was

startled when he spoke again, 'I'm glad you turned back. . . I wish I could have. . . long ago. . .'

And with that, he died.

I stood up slowly, my heart heavy for a man I had known for a long time. Dash had been kindly disposed towards me and I had enjoyed his company. I was grieved by his dying.

'The other one's getting away,' came a yell from further down the tunnel, and I left the medics to take care of Dash's body while I resumed the chase.

I was now at the rear of the pursuit, running beside Pop, who was not so young or so fit as the others.

Soon we came to the end of the sewer where, beyond the giant circle of the entrance, could be seen the moonlit waters of the harbour.

Captain Metellus and his officers concluded that Camillus had hidden himself in one of the side tunnels.

'Back up the tunnel, men!' ordered Metellus. 'Spread out and search thoroughly.'

Pop and I left them to their task.

'These old lungs are out of breath.' complained Pop, 'I must find a place to sit down and rest.'

I led him out into the fresh night air, filled with the salty tang of the ocean, where we sat down on the rocks that surrounded the entrance to the sewer.

'How did you know that Camillus was the Falcon?' I asked.

'For a long time I did not know,' replied Pop, 'and when I had finally deduced the real identity of the Falcon, sadly, I was unaware that you were considering a job offer from him. If I had known I would have warned you.'

'Yeah, I should have told you,' I admitted. 'But what put you on to his trail?'

'Thinking, just thinking. Using, as one of my

distinguished colleagues in the detective business occasionally says, the little grey cells. The more I thought about what you had told me about Mr Publius Camillus the more puzzled I became.'

'Puzzled? By what?'

'By the thought of him running a detective agency. He is, as you yourself pointed out, a Roman nobleman. What is a member of a wealthy noble family doing running a detective agency?'

'Hey! That's right! Those noble families are big landowners. And they never go in for dirtying their hands with grubby commerce.'

'My thoughts exactly,' said Pop. 'So I began to wonder about Mr Camillus. And as I wondered I remembered what Cassandra had said. You'll remember her telling us that she once worked for a noble Roman family who lost their money in foolish investments. If that was Camillus's family, it would explain why Camillus had to go into business. It would also explain how he came to know Cassandra and her peculiar talents. It would also explain why he chose to go into such an unlikely business as running a detective agency: as the perfect cover for Falcon Incorporated. He was the Falcon's "head", the planner and organiser—while Cassandra was the Falcon's "hand", carrying out the plans he made.'

'And it was Camillus who murdered Mr Cairo?'

'Precisely, since it would have been Camillus who approached Mr Cairo to obtain employment for Cassandra at the palace.'

'Why did he do it, Pop? Why would someone born with all the advantages that Camillus was born with, become a professional assassin?'

'We shall probably never know. Perhaps he was embittered by his family's loss of wealth and fortune.

Perhaps he believed that, because of his noble birth, the world owed him a living. Perhaps he simply chose the path of evil.'

For a while we sat in silence while I absorbed these thoughts, then I became aware of sounds coming from the small beach beyond the rocks.

'Listen!' I said. 'What's that?'

In the next moment we knew exactly what it was. The splashing and bumping noises were swamped by a sudden roar as a powerful motor boat thundered into life, and Pop and I scrambled over the rocks towards the sound.

We arrived on the beach to find Camillus steering his boat out onto the harbour. He must have escaped from the sewers through another exit a little further up.

He must have seen us in the silvery-blue moonlight, for he shut the throttle down, stood up in the boat and called out.

'You'll hear from me again, Ben Bartholomew. You'll hear from me again!'

Then he sat down, opened the throttle up full, and disappeared across the harbour.

I immediately ran off in search of Captain Metellus. But by the time I had found him, and he had alerted the harbour patrol, and the harbour patrol had got their search boat out, it was too late. Camillus had gained the safety of his yacht, the *M.V. Victorius* had weighed anchor, and was steaming out to sea at full speed.

'No sign of Camillus yet?' asked Tim.

'Not so far,' replied Commander Cornelius, 'But he

will be caught—eventually. You can rest assured of that.'

It was the day following our pursuit of the Falcon, and we were all gathered in Paul's room at the palace.

I was somewhat embarrassed to realise that the gathering was a 'welcome to the family' party—for me.

Tim had thrown an arm around my shoulders and told me how delighted he was that I had made my decision, Paul had taken me to one side and given me a lot of excellent advice, and even Doctor Lucas, who could be rather quiet and reserved, was full of smiles and welcomes for the 'new Christian.'

Earlier Mom had been delighted by the same news, and never stopped telling everyone how long she and Pop had been praying for me, and how pleased they were.

Later, as we were walking back from the palace I said to Pop, 'Well, I guess I'd better knuckle down to my legal studies now.'

'If you do so I shall be delighted,' said Pop. 'But that is not the big issue. What really matters, is your standing before God, and your eternal destiny. And that is what I am so pleased about right now.'

'I'm pleased you're pleased, Pop,' I said. 'You know something?'

'What?'

'You really are quite a guy, Pop. And not a bad detective either!'

'For these flattering words, many thanks. But you would please me if you would follow my wishes in one small matter.'

'Anything at all. What is it, Pop?'

'Don't call me Pop!'

From Mystery to History

The original murder plot: Although the investigations of Sam and Ben Bartholomew in *The Case of the Secret Assassin* are pure fiction, they were inspired by a real murder plot. In 57AD, just 24 years after the death and resurrection of Jesus, Paul of Tarsus arrived in Jerusalem, accompanied by a group of his friends including some Greeks, and carrying with him a sum of money he had collected amongst his Asian churches to help the poor Christians of Jerusalem.

The Christian leaders in that city were anxious that Paul demonstrate to the Jewish Christians that he still respected their traditions. They suggested that he join with, and sponsor, a group of four men who were about to devote a week to special religious observations at the Temple. Paul agreed.

When that week was almost up some Jews from Turkey (Asia Minor) spotted Paul at the Temple and accused him of bringing non-Jews into an area from which they were strictly prohibited. These Turkish Jews were old enemies of Paul's because he had travelled through their region preaching and converting many to Christianity.

The charge they brought may have been due to an honest error: they may have seen Paul with his Greek friends and assumed that he had also brought them into the Temple. Or it may have been a malicious invention.

Either way, the result was a riot from which the Roman soldiers had to rescue Paul, and which, in turn led to the murder plot recorded in the prologue to this book. (If you would like to know more about the historical background of the New Testament the best introduction is a book called *From Bethlehem to Patmos* by Paul Barnett.)

Paul of Tarsus: Tarsus was a town on the Cilician plain ten miles inland from the south coast of modern Turkey. In New Testament times it was an important university town with a population of half a million, and a place where Eastern and Western cultures met. An important city, anyone born in Tarsus automatically had Roman citizenship.

Paul was named 'Saul' when he was born in Tarsus—the year of his birth being unknown. He received his tertiary education under Rabbi Gamaliel in Jerusalem.

Paul, or Saul as he was then, was a Pharisee bitterly opposed to the Christians, who took an active part in the early persecution of the church.

He was on his way to Damascus to arrest the Christians there when he saw a dazzling light and heard the voice of the resurrected Jesus speak to him. He was converted, his name changed to Paul, and he became, in time, one of the great teachers and preachers of the Christian faith.

Paul travelled around a great deal of the ancient world taking the message of Christianity especially to non-Jewish people. In the New Testament there is a section called 'Acts' which records many of his activities.

His letters to the churches he founded made up a large part of the New Testament.

The most important of Paul's letters is the one he wrote the Roman Christians. You'll find it in the New Testament under heading 'Romans': I recommend reading it in a clear, easy-to-read modern translation of the Bible. (You'll find an excellent guide to Paul's letter to the Romans in a book called *How to Be a Christian Without Being Religious* by Fritz Ridenour.)

Governor Felix: Marcus Antonius Felix was a brother of Pallas who was, in turn, a favourite of the Emperor Claudius. Through this influence, Felix was appointed Governor (or Procurator) of the province of Judaea.

It was before Felix that Paul stood trial in Caesarea. The governor kept Paul imprisoned for two years (AD 57-59), hoping for a bribe. When his replacement, a man named Porcius Festus, arrived the Jews again applied to have Paul transferred back to Jerusalem. Their plan was to make a second attempt to ambush and murder Paul.

243

Paul responded by exercising his right as a Roman citizen of appealing directly to the Emperor for judgement. The result was that in AD 59, Paul, still a prisoner in chains and under guard, set sail for Rome.

Doctor Lucas: The man called Luke by the the New Testament (I call him 'Doctor Lucas' in the story) was a Greek-speaking non-Jew, who was probably born in the city of Antioch. Luke wrote two of the sections of the New Testament: the one which bears his name (which is a biographical study of Jesus) and the one called 'Acts' which records the history of the spread of Christianity throughout the Roman Empire, and especially the work of Paul.

Very little is known about Luke. We know from his writings that he was a well-educated man and a thorough and careful historian. Scholars have described his as one of the most reliable historians of antiquity. (If you'd like to know about the reliability of Luke and the other Biblical historians I recommend a book called *Is the New Testament History?* by Paul Barnett.)

Luke is a humble and disciplined writer who keeps himself in the background, hence there is little more that we know, except that he was trained as a physician, and that he was one of Paul's most loyal and faithful friends.

Jerusalem: In AD 57 Jerusalem was a great Jewish city and religious centre, but it was under the direct rule and control of the Romans.

The Temple, which was the largest building in the city, stood on a hill in eastern Jerusalem. West and north of the Temple lay a small area of shops, stores and houses. The Old Wall encircled most of southern Jerusalem. A short jagged wall cut across this area and separated it into the parts called the Lower City and the Upper City.

The crowded Lower City, east of the jagged wall, was the commercial and industrial centre of Jerusalem and the chief residential area of its poor. Most of Jerusalem's wealthy people lived in the Upper City, which included King Herod's Jerusalem palace and many large homes with spacious courtyards, gardens and pools.

Immediately north of the Temple was the Fortress Antonia. This was the Roman military headquarters in Jerusalem, and it was here that Paul was held in protective custody until he was hurried away under armed guard to Caesarea.

Caesarea: Caesarea was a Mediterranean port city built by Herod the Great (born 73 BC, died 4 BC). Herod named the place after the Roman Emperor Augustus Caesar, and statues of the emperor stood in a huge temple dedicated to him and to Rome.

Caesarea stood on one of the great caravan routes, making it a centre for inland as well as coastal trade. To make the port safer for sea-going vessels Herod had elaborate stone breakwaters erected to the north and south of the harbour.

Caesarea was lavishly adorned with palaces, public buildings, and an enormous amphitheatre. Herod built himself a grand summer palace in the city, and it was this palace that became the home of later Roman governors, and the place where Paul was imprisoned.

Pharisee: The word Pharisee probably means 'separated ones'. They were a strict religious sect who kept closely to the Jewish Law.

Pharisees insisted upon: the unity and holiness of God; that Israel was God's chosen people; and that the Jewish Law was absolutely authoritative. Beyond this, however, the Pharisee's religion was ethical not theological.

Paul was raised as a Pharisee and trained by one of their great leaders. The Pharisees were always a minority sect: at the time when our story is set there may have been around 6,000 of them.

Sadducees: This group was smaller than the Pharisees but more influential. Most Sadducees were members of wealthy, noble Jewish families.

The Sadducees tended to be close to the seat of power, gladly co-operating with their Roman conquerors in return for retaining some powers of government over the city of Jerusalem. Most of the historical records of the Sadducees were written by their enemies and describe them as snobbish and arrogant, being rude

245

to other Jews as well as foreigners, and regarding it as a virtue to argue with their teachers.

In religion the Sadducees were conservative. They denied the validity of any but the very earliest written laws, and rejected the doctrines of the soul, its after-life, the resurrection, rewards and retribution, angels and demons.

The Sadducees were Paul's enemies.

Cornelius: Cornelius was a common name in the Roman world, ever since Publius Cornelius Sulla liberated 10,000 slaves in 82 BC. The Cornelius we read about in the New Testament (Acts) was a captain (or centurion) in the Roman army based in Caesarea.

This Cornelius is significant as being the first non-Jew ever to become a Christian. This happened in response to the preaching of Peter not very long after the death and resurrection of Jesus.

For the purposes of my story I have imagined Cornelius more than twenty years later, promoted to the rank of commander, and still one of the leading lights in the Christian church in Caesarea.

Philip: Although he plays only a very small part in our story, Philip actually played a very important part in bringing Christianity to Caesarea.

He was originally an official (called a 'deacon') in the Christian church in Jerusalem. He then became an 'evangelist' (one who spreads the good news of Christianity). After a number of travels and adventures he ended up in the major port city of Caesarea where he appears to have settled down and established the local Christian church.

More than twenty years later we know that he was still in Caesarea where Paul stayed with him on the journey to Jerusalem that ended in imprisonment. For the purposes of my story I have imagined Philip to be the pastor of the local church (which, in all likelihood, he was).

The Logic of the Universe: The pilgrimage of Sam Bartholomew recorded in *The Case of the Secret Assassin* involves Sam coming face to face with what Ben calls 'the logic of the universe'. Over the past two thousand years many millions of people have had the same experience—I know because I am one of them.

The experience involves facing up to the reality of God, and the necessity of responding to him—either with acceptance or rejection. In Sam's journey you'll notice that there are six clear stages:

1   It begins with creation. Sam was confronted with God's ownership (God's rule) of the whole of creation, and, as a result, our dependence on God. Sam had to recognise his relationship to God as being that of a creature to a loving Creator. Everything we are and everything we possess comes from God. Failure comes from trying to declare our independence and self-government.

2   Such declarations of independence, such rebellion, is what is meant by the old-fashioned word 'sin'. Sam discovered that any attempt at self-government is a crime against our Maker and Owner, because we are part of his creation and are accountable to him.

3   Once Sam could understand his rebellion against God's ownership, he could also see judgement as the logical consequence. The justice of God's judgement is seen once we understand the enormity of our crime. We have defied God's ownership and have chosen other gods—ourselves!

4   Our problem is that we are under the judgement of God—and it is God himself who provides the solution for our problem! Sam learned that God's Son, Jesus, became a human and lived a perfect life so that he could take the punishment which humans deserve. Sam discovered that God's act of sending his Son, Jesus, to die for sinful humans was sheer mercy—an act of astonishing generosity which applied to him personally.

5   The resurrection of Jesus, his conquest of death, is part of this whole story: as the Son of God death could not hold him, God raised him, and so opened the way through death for all who follow him. Furthermore, this resurrection is God's statement that Jesus is his chosen and appointed Ruler of this world.

6   The crunch came for Sam in confronting his own need to respond to this good news. He realised that he needed 'faith' (that simply means *trust* in Jesus as his rescuer and ruler); and he

247

needed 'repentance' (that simply means *turning around*—saying 'I was living my life that way, now I will live it this way').

The key to all of this, in Sam's life as in yours and mine, is to ask God to change us so that we can admit that 'Jesus is Lord' and can follow and serve him as such.

Who Moved the Stone?

Frank Morison

'. . . The third day he rose again from the dead . . .'

This famous book is addressed to the momentous question: What really happened between the arrest of Jesus in the garden of Gethsemane and the discovery of the empty tomb?

'Fascinating in its lucid, its almost incontrovertible, appeal to the reason.'
— *J.D. Beresford*

'It is as though a skilled advocate, entirely convinced of the truth of his case, were unravelling the threads of some mystery . . . It has the supreme merit of frankness and sincerity.'
— *The Sunday Times*

ISBN 0-903843-75-7

publishing
CARLISLE, UK

Christianity is Ridiculous
Eighty Big Objections to Believing a Word of It

John Allan

'If God knew we would make a mess of this planet, it was irresponsible of him to create it.'

'Jesus and his earliest followers may have been clever frauds.'

'Some books of the Bible disagree with others.'

'All religions lead to God: the church has no monopoly.'

This is a new edition of *Express Checkout*, the classic which came out of John Allan and Guy Eyre's 'Express Checkout' programme at Greenbelt, designed to help people understand Christian basics.

Comprehensive and user-friendly, the book is made up of eight sections: questions about God, about Jesus, about the Bible, about the church, about conversion, about life and death, about world problems and tragedies, and about being a Christian.

ISBN 1-85078-136-2

OM publishing
CARLISLE, UK

Christianity is Impossible
Eighty Big Problems in Living Life as a Christian

John Allan

Following the same style as *Christianity is Ridiculous*, and as comprehensive and user-friendly, the book is made up of eight sections: questions about prayer, about the Bible, about sharing your faith, about the church, about relationships, about standards, about puzzles and dilemmas, and about the rest of the world.

'Why is prayer so difficult?'

'I never read anything—why should I read the Bible?'

'Why are there so many hypocrites in the church?'

'Is Christianity anti-feminist?'

ISBN 1-85078-140-0

M publishing
CARLISLE, UK

OM PUBLISHING

OM Publishing specializes in popular paperbacks in three vital areas of the church's work:

EVANGELISM
DISCIPLESHIP
MISSION

In addition, OM Publishing spearheaded the 'Pray for the World' campaign, led by the titles *Operation World* and *You Can Change the World*.

For a free catalogue, write now to:

OM Publishing, PO Box 300, Carlisle, Cumbria CA3 0QS, UK.

publishing
CARLISLE, UK